CANDLELIGHT ROMANCES

SEARCH FOR YESTERDAY

Barbara Doyle

A CANDLELIGHT ROMANCE

Published by
Dell Publishing Co., Inc.
1 Dag Hammarskjold Plaza
New York, New York 10017

Dell ® TM 681510, Dell Publishing Co., Inc.

ISBN: 0-440-18297-2

Printed in the United States of America

First printing—September 1979

SEARCH FOR
YESTERDAY

CHAPTER 1

Ellen remembered the uneasy feeling she had before boarding the train in Madrid an hour earlier. She wondered then if it could have been an omen of an ill-fated journey yet to come. But with a deep breath she had boarded anyway and proceeded to settle herself uncomfortably against the once plush blue-velvet seat now dingy and frayed—and in her mind—as dismal as the rest of that vehicle that was making its eight-hour journey south to Seville in the Andalusian province.

A previous urge of extravagance to rent a car for the trip should not have been overlooked, she thought. If the last hour exemplified the rest of the journey, it was sure to be a drab and tiresome ride. The air in the coach had already become heavy with dust, and the window at her side was streaked with a muddled combination of dirt on dried raindrops—giving evidence that the train had traveled a less arid route than the flat *mancha* which now surrounded it. Yet she knew that those windows were her only escape from the dreariness that she felt, and she continued to stare through them at the vastness of red earth that was once the highway of Cervantes's dreams. Here the author had manipulated Don Quixote through his various escapades. It would not have surprised her to see the humble silhouette of the hunched and docile Sancho Panza hovering by the side of the small whitewashed buildings that lined the flag stops.

The excitement that began to mount in her at the thought of being in the center of the area depicted in one of the greatest pieces of literature was short-lived. She remembered suddenly that this trip would not be like others she had taken in the last three years. Sandy was gone from her life, and she could no longer look forward to ravenously taking in all of her surroundings with the explicit goal of writing him each night. She remembered sending him avid descriptions of what she had seen on her journeys. He was gone from her life now, and the void that he had once filled was still giving her pangs of loneliness that hurt terribly. She could see him so clearly at that moment, with his ruddy abundance of hair that was so easily tousled by the slightest hint of wind. Gone also was the comfortable and easy personality, the understanding nature, and the ever-present willingness to guide her through every step of her life. Of course it was this last that became so stifling and so complicating to the relationship. How could he understand that she had to breathe? Why couldn't he understand that being able to breathe did not necessarily mean a failing of her love? So they had parted, and the parting was tragic but inevitable—and now she was alone.

Little towns had begun to spring up more frequently as the train sped toward the fringe of the *mancha* and her mental hiatus was broken. As some of the buildings and hills cut the sun's direct rays from the train, Ellen caught a glimpse of herself in the window and she was not pleased at what she saw. Her usual shining dark hair was tossed and dingy, and there were smudges on her face that obstructed her usually clear, olive skin. But, she thought she looked no worse than the other riders in the train who alternated the afternoon's activities between cooling themselves with makeshift fans and opening small parcels of homemade nourishment. She found everything about the journey drab and uncomfortable and again wondered if this was a prophecy of what she was to encounter in San Juan Aznalfarache, which was to be her journey's end.

Now the red-baked crust of hills began to loom higher, taking the place of the flat *mancha*. As the heat of the day increased, the hills seemed to close in and stifle the train. She took another deep sigh and decided that there was no more to do but sit back in her seat and close her eyes. Perhaps sleep would pass the time quickly for her. But, alas, sleep did not come.

She reprimanded herself quietly for being so restless and discontent with the trip. Hadn't Jim Bradley done her a favor by giving this assignment to her? A trip to Spain paid for by the museum was nothing to be annoyed by.

Jim had received the letter three weeks before. The Pedregal family had two paintings that they felt sure were Enrique Perez originals. The Cordobés painter was renowned for his exquisite and sensitive work depicting Andalusian women. The

Pedregal museum had a good collection of Spanish paintings plus various inlaid furniture and
gold jewelry from the Spain of ancient times. Jim
was requested to send an art appraiser and histo-
rian to the Pedregal villa to authenticate the
paintings. The request also contained an additional assignment of searching for and authenti-
cating the original documents of the artwork. The
family specifically wanted the work done through
a museum in the States. To bypass close acquaintances in Spain? . . . for prestige? She
wasn't sure, but the request did come in.

She had almost begged Jim to give her the assignment of documenting the paintings. And he,
being the sensitive old father figure that he was to
all of his staff, had realized her upset in breaking
with Sandy and agreed to let her go. Keep in
touch, he had said. Do your work, but forget everything here. Wallow in the sunshine and get
some of that old-world charm into your veins.

Oh, Jim, she thought, did we do the right thing
by sending me here to strange surroundings?
Shouldn't I be surrounded by friends consoling
me, rationalizing with me that I did the right
thing in breaking up with Sandy?

She knew the answer to those questions before
they even left her head. She needed time for
healing and she had to do this on her own. Her
friends couldn't help her this time. How could
they know how deep the void was. Most of them
had not gone through a similar experience. How
could they, who had yet to taste the bitterness of
life's tragedies, really know what she was going

through? She was again annoyed at herself in realizing that her split with Sandy had opened Pandora's box of troubled thoughts so that everything had to be pondered and weighed before any move, even simple, was made. Perhaps this assignment would be good for her after all.

Her reverie was broken again. The man in the dark suit across the aisle suddenly rose from his seat to gather a large briefcase from the overhead shelf. His movements distracted her from her own thoughts, and she was grateful for this.

She looked out of the window again and realized that dusk had replaced the hot rays of sun and that the first part of her journey in Spain would soon come to an end. There were no hills now, but the earth suddenly exploded with very tall foliage that was so lush it seemed hard to remember the vacuous, red earth of the earlier hours. She looked again to her right at the gentleman who was still collecting his belongings. She had noticed him at intervals during the day working over a mass of papers. For some reason he was too formal and proper in appearance to be taking this uncomfortable ride. She could better place him at the airport or in a car-rental office than sitting on that dust-catching vehicle. She made her choice only to assimilate some of the flavor of the countryside without bothering to drive herself.

At any rate, she reminded herself that she was on this journey to do a good job on the assignment and that all personal problems should be pushed aside as much as possible.

* * *

The station cleared rapidly, and for a moment Ellen thought she would be stranded without transportation to the villa. Madama Pedregal had clearly stated in her letter to Jim Bradley that someone would be there to meet Ellen. She wondered what this woman would be like, insisting on using the antiquated title of "Madama." Eccentric? Pompous? From royalty? No matter. She dismissed the thought and was walking toward the exit when she saw the bent old man running toward her and waving his arms frantically.

"No doubt you are headed for the Pedregal villa. You are Señorita Ross, and I'm to take you. Come, give me your cases."

Without waiting for an answer he cupped her two bags under one of his arms, while the other took her elbow as she was gently, but firmly urged around the corner.

"The doctor is already in the carriage," his chatter continued. "Joaquin is in Málaga with the car, but this will do nicely. The trip is short from here, and the jasmine is out. You will like it," he seemed to decide.

Ellen's eyes widened. Surely the man must be a little mad. But, in another thought, she welcomed this odd little person who had left her no time to feather any apprehensions of whether this journey and assignment were right for her at this time in her personal life. There was certainly a carriage standing at the curb near the side of the station entrance, and as she boarded it, a gentleman, already seated, rose to give her adequate room. To her surprise it was the passenger she had noticed on the train.

"Doctor, this is Señorita Ross. She has come to document the paintings," said the old man.

"Doctor Bradshaw," the man nodded. His large blue eyes penetrated her own so deeply that she felt herself coloring slightly. Yet his expression was stern, almost showing annoyance.

"You mustn't mind old Felix," he continued. "His efficiency sometimes becomes overwhelming. But things get done and that gives one a feeling of security in these parts." With that he turned his head away to look out the opposite side of the carriage and proceeded to dismiss Ellen completely, as if satisfied that the beginning amenities were over and done with and he was relieved.

Somewhat abashed, she said, "I do hope that my presence is not inconveniencing you. I could wait for other transportation." The flippancy in her voice even startled herself, but she felt he had dismissed her and she was too tired and in no mood to take that from this haughty gentleman. She was a little shaky about this entire venture, but she was not about to be pushed aside and to take it lightly. There, she felt more of her stability returning. Anger sometimes helped her fears to take second place. Besides, the man began to intrigue her and she wanted to keep him talking.

"You are not inconveniencing me," he was saying. Again his eyes met hers, but now they seemed to soften. His grin was that of a child who was made to feel sheepish for being called down

by an elder for ill manners. Ellen felt herself really coloring now as she viewed him face on. She
had already noticed his wavy black hair on the
train, but his smile, slightly crooked and almost
wicked, lighted his face and made him most appealing.

"Besides," he continued, "there would be no
other transportation to the villa, and it would be
wasteful to expect Felix to return to transport us
individually, wouldn't it?" The grin was gone
now, as his face resumed an expression of
parental authority. Yet his eyes still lingered on
her face a few moments more, and then as they
traveled quickly over the rest of her body, she realized that he had taken in everything about her
in the last few seconds.

"You are a stranger to these parts, Miss Ross?
Are you here for romance, or adventure—or is it
both?" he continued.

She made her voice stiff to show her contempt
for his questioning as she answered, "Neither,
Doctor. I'm here on assignment—to do a job and to
leave soon after I've completed it."

"You're certainly very dedicated to your work
to arrive in late August to Spain's own inferno.
From what you say then you have not met
Joaquin yet?"

"Joaquin? No," she answered sullenly. "I know
no one in the Pedregal family. As I said, I'm on
assignment."

There was an obvious silence between them,
but he soon covered it.

"Perhaps you have also come to see the bulls. This area is the mecca of bullfighting and of the bull-breeding ranches. The *fincas* established around Seville feed the bullrings of the entire country."

"I've never seen a bullfight."

"Then we must plan to see one together," he was saying.

She would do nothing of the sort, she thought. She hoped she would not be seeing much of this man, whose very gaze and varied moods unnerved her in some way that she could not comprehend. She did not yet know Dr. Bradshaw's connection with the villa, but he was beginning to dampen her spirit which was not too strong anyway.

The carriage careened across a tiny bridge, guarded by two ancient towers left over from the glorious Golden Age of Spain. The black river below sparkled with fireflies as the café lights and lanterns along the river bank reflected in its waters. The scent of jasmine filled her nostrils, sweet and intoxicating. For a moment Ellen leaned back in the carriage and let the aura of gaiety direct her into a false moment of enchantment, molding her companion into the legendary prince come to take her into a land of love and peace. But it was truly a moment of escape, as she could already see stretches of barren, black road ahead through the lacings of the trees, a road that seemed so dark it could almost be touched—one that led to further darkness and the unknown. She shivered.

"Are you cold, Miss Ross?"

"Just tired, I think," she answered. She felt loneliness engulf her again. She was certainly batting zero when the very first person she contacted since her arrival already was at odds with her. Perhaps she was too quick to leave Sandy. Was there ever to be someone in this world as kind as he had been?

"Doctor, we approach your chalet. The carriage ride was pleasant." It was Felix again, breaking her thoughts. Felix, who was not only efficient, but optimistic. She agreed. The carriage ride was not uncomfortable. The horses were reined to the right, and there, not far from the road and immersed in palm, honeysuckle, and jasmine, stood a little blue stucco house. The prince's chalet, Ellen thought. But he was to walk in alone, and she, the princess, was to be led away.

"The lights are on. Milta must have received my message." The doctor jumped out of the carriage, and after gathering his briefcase and small overnight bag, he surprised her by taking her hand. Nothing was said for a few moments, and she felt her own speech paralyzed by confusion.

"If you are intent on weathering the heat and remaining here, Miss Ross, then we will be seeing much of each other. Since I'm only renting the chalet from the Pedregals for a few months, Joaquin insists that I take dinner at the villa. Milta is adequate for cleaning and maintaining general order at the chalet, but she has no finesse in cooking. We'll talk further on the merits of southern Spain in August and the fascination of the bullring." With that, he turned and walked toward the chalet.

"Ahhhhh," Felix was alerting the horses, and the carriage made an abrupt start. As she turned her head, she noticed the doctor standing in front of the entry gates of the chalet watching the carriage drive off.

It was obvious that he thought of her as a foolish tourist on a spree in a strange country. Yet somewhere in his manner he was taunting her presence there at all, as if he were warning her against something. And who was this Joaquin whom the doctor assumed she already knew?

Enough worrying and questioning, she thought. The day had been long and unnerving, and with that she sat back in the carriage, folded her hands in her lap, and allowed Felix to drive her the remaining distance to the villa.

CHAPTER 2

The large house was situated about two hundred yards from the doctor's chalet and practically hidden from the road by an immense garden, similar in context to the doctor's, but more dense. The two-story villa was painted brown and contained three entry arches designed in such a fashion that they reminded Ellen of three human frowns. To the left of the building, and appearing very much like an afterthought to the original structure, was a tall tower with a painted roof, without giving any clue to its usefulness. To the right of the entrance stood another addition, but this was a small rectangular building that Ellen guessed might house the servant staff.

"You are in awe, señorita?" asked Felix as he produced an oversized key and began opening the ornately carved doors to the villa.

"It is magnificent. A glory from another time," she answered quietly.

They stepped through the entry which took them into a typical Spanish courtyard, still and mysterious, yet crying loudly of its varied history. The center of the garden was splattered with palms, and brightly hued flowers were placed at intervals around a magnificent fountain. The house seemed uninhabited, and only the trickle of water from the fountain harmonized with the gentle swish of palm leaves moving slowly in the warm breeze. The patio was dimly lit with white and green lights thoughtfully placed behind the palm stalks so that the rays of light that touched the leaves seemed to have grown with the trees themselves.

"What a marvelous study, Felix," she sighed, feeling, for the first time since her arrival, an enthusiasm over her assignment.

"You will do it, then, señorita? You will say nice things about the paintings for Señor Joaquin then?" he stammered.

She looked at the man curiously before answering, "I'll appraise the paintings as accurately as possible, Felix. And I'm sure that Joaquin will be pleased." She wondered if this was the type of answer the man was seeking.

Her eye caught the two paintings in the foyer. She would study them at length later. She began to stroll around the patio, quietly giving reverence to the surroundings. Felix remained still, allowing her to do so without any further interference as if realizing the deep effect the place had on her.

She looked up and noticed that a tarpaulin covered one quarter of the ceiling area of the patio, and the rest was left to the open sky. The courtyard itself was framed with Moorish-shaped arches lining a covered passageway. Here the walls were done in Andalusian tile, ornately designed with wine-colored floral prints. These tiles covered most of the floor area also, with only a few tapestry carpets interrupting their pattern.

The upper tier along the patio seemed to contain the family's living quarters, and as Ellen's eyes searched the area, she noticed a figure of a woman descending the staircase to the garden, her long robe floating over the steps while her gaze never left the new intruders to her household.

The figure was closer now and Ellen noticed that it was a slender young woman in her middle-twenties.

"You are Miss Ross?" Her voice was arrogant. "Señor Joaquin is away, and Madama retired early to her quarters. Come, I will show you to your room." With that she picked up Ellen's two cases and proceeded to carry them across the courtyard and up the steps. Since Felix made no protest to stop her, Ellen decided to let the gesture go without comment, although the custom was quite unfamiliar to her.

She was being dismissed again, she thought. Was this all the greeting she was to receive after such a long journey?

"I'll try not to inconvenience anyone while I'm here," she ventured.

"My instructions were to tell you to feel free to wander about the premises at will," the girl answered, her voice still chilled.

Surprisingly to Ellen, the accommodations she was shown were on the second level of the house overlooking the courtyard. The room itself was very large and at one end contained a four-poster bed with two side tables. At the other corner of the room someone had arranged a sitting area, with chaise longue, soft chair, and desk ensemble.

"Would you care for me to unpack for you, Miss Ross?" The girl had placed the bags in front of the bed and stood gazing at Ellen, her eyes piercing with hostility.

"No, I'll tend to that," she almost snapped, but contained herself in enough time so that the words came out softly.

"I'm Louisa—housekeeper here," she continued. "If there is anything you need, you will pull the cord, and I or Ana will tend to your needs."

"Yes, you could do me one favor," Ellen said. "You seem to look at me as if . . . as if we have either met before, or you were not expecting me. Is there something wrong, Louisa?"

"Nothing, señorita. Of course we expected you. It's just . . . well, I was expecting another type . . . an older person."

"Don't worry, please. My appraising abilities will do the paintings justice. I'm not an amateur in the field," laughed Ellen.

"Yes, señorita. I'll have Ana serve you some dinner here in your room. Oh—breakfast tomorrow will be in the *antesala* at your leisure. The family will expect you for dinner tomorrow evening at eight." With that she took her leave.

Ellen slumped exhaustedly on the bed, the letdown of all her anticipations leaving her drained. Not one of the people she had met thus far seemed to want her there, except Felix—and she was sure he would be optimistic about anything. No matter, she thought, there was nothing to do now but unpack and make the best of it.

She looked around her room. It was cheery

enough with a floral-print bedspread of pink and green that matched the draperies. The scattered rugs were like islands of lily pads against the solid wood floors. The ornately carved wood of the ceiling and door made the atmosphere quite elegant.

As she began unpacking her things, she thought of Dr. Bradshaw again. What a very negative man, she mused, and while she did so, she felt her face flushing.

He was annoyed at her presence there, but she couldn't understand why. He seemed to be a very formal man. Perhaps that was why he had no patience with what he assumed to be young maidens traveling without purpose through foreign countries. In thinking of him she was sorry that she had met him so soon into her trip. What she needed now was to be surrounded by pleasant people. She needed solace for her breakup with Sandy. Or did she? Dr. Bradshaw had taken her mind off Sandy in the last hour. But she didn't need that type of distraction, she trusted. Not from that negative man.

She busied herself unpacking her things, feeling relief that she didn't have to meet the family that evening. It was at that moment that she thought she heard a cry of sorts coming from somewhere on the landing. Looking up, she realized that her door had not been tightly closed. Without hesitating she made her way to the landing and followed the muffled sounds as closely as possible.

The door where they emanated was also slightly ajar, and as she approached it, she could see a child curled into a round heap on her bed, sobbing into her pillow.

Ellen entered very quietly, trying not to frighten the kittenlike creature.

"Hello, there," she said. "Have you had a bad dream?"

The child turned over slightly and peered at her through one opened eye, as if still keeping the other closed for security against the unknown.

"Who are you?" she whimpered. "You must be another friend of my father's." With that she placed her head back into the pillows and began to sob again.

"Don't be afraid. I won't hurt you," answered Ellen. "As a matter of fact, I'm not a friend of your father's. Sadly enough, I have no friends here at all," she continued, making a mental note of how true that statement really was.

The child's sobbing quieted a little as she turned again toward Ellen. "You don't have any friends—not even one?" she gasped.

"Not a one. As a matter of fact, it feels quite strange being in a country that is unfamiliar to me."

"Well," answered the child, "I'm not in a strange country, but I do know how you feel being without friends. I don't have any either." Here her voice began to catch again.

"I'm sure you have lots of friends," Ellen said, trying her best to be reassuring.

"No, none at all, anymore. I used to have some. My mother . . . my mother used to take me to visit them before she . . . before she had to go away. My mother is in heaven, you see," she said quite soberly for her years.

"I see," said Ellen, regretting bitterly that she had pursued the topic.

"I'm sure you have friends that you see at school," she added.

"Most of them go to the sea in the summer. We used to do that at one time. My father is so busy with the ranch, and my grandmother does not like the sea at all. She always stays at the villa. She told me once that she loves the villa more than anything else in the world. That's why she doesn't take me to the sea," she said.

"I'm sure that once school starts you'll be seeing your friends again," Ellen added.

"Oh, yes. I'm looking forward to that," answered the child as she eyed the girl curiously. "What is your name?" she then asked.

"My name is Ellen Ross. I'm here to appraise some very fine paintings that your father owns."

"Miss Ross, if you really feel very lonely being here, I could be your friend," the child said.

"Well, that would be marvelous. As a matter of fact, I was wondering something myself. Since Seville is new to me, I not only get a chance to do my work but also to take in the sights as if I were on vacation. But there is only one thing wrong."

"And what is that?"

"I really don't want to just wander around the city aimlessly when I have some free time. I'd like to know what I'm looking at. I wonder . . . if you're not too busy with other things, would you like to be my guide?"

The eyes that were so red and moist with sadness when Ellen had entered the room suddenly widened with such happiness that she could not stifle a grateful chuckle.

"Do you really mean that?" the child asked.

"Yes, I do . . . if it won't be too much trouble," she restated soberly.

"Of course it wouldn't," the child said as she sat up completely in bed. Ellen noticed the beautiful silky black hair and wide dark eyes. She guessed that the child was about eight or nine.

"Only one thing," said Ellen. "If you are going to be my official guide, I think I should know your name."

"Oh, I completely forgot to introduce myself," the child said, now bending forward and back in convulsive laughter. "My name is Amparo," she finally managed. "And my father's name is Joaquin. Joaquin Pedregal. He is the owner here. Well, he and my grandmother, that is."

"I am happy to know you, Amparo," Ellen said as she extended her hand to the child. "Now, before I tuck you in for the night, I would like to give you your first assignment. I don't think I could start my research on the paintings unless I see some of the area. Would you like to accompany me to town tomorrow and show me a few of the sights?"

"Oh I would be happy to do that," Amparo answered, beaming with happiness.

"Well, let's both get some sleep then." With that she covered the child and kissed her cheek, which was sticky where the earlier tears had left their marks. Her long black hair smothered the pillow as she took tight hold of Ellen's hand and tried to sleep. Soon the grip relaxed, and her eyelids fluttered and then closed.

Ellen stood and looked at the sleeping figure for a few minutes. She had a beautiful little face with perfect features, and Ellen knew that the tears had come from sheer loneliness.

As she walked back to her room she realized that with all the new surroundings and equally new faces, she had not thought of Sandy once since she had disembarked from the train. She didn't know if she would ever get used to anyone there. Louisa was so cool and distant, and Dr. Bradshaw—again at the thought of him she felt her face warm but fought against the feeling. Dr. Bradshaw was pompous and nasty, she finished. Of course there was Felix, who she was sure she would not be seeing too often, and Amparo. Thankfully, she thought, she had met Amparo.

As she entered her room and pulled down the bedclothes she remembered one other. What of Joaquin? she thought. What would he be like?

With all of these characters spinning in her head she went to sleep. At first it was a restless sleep, and then, as exhaustion overruled, a deep, dreamless sleep until morning.

CHAPTER 3

Ellen had never seen a street so narrow. She felt as though she could touch one storefront with her left hand and still reach the other side of the street with her right. Calle Sierpes was truly the street of the snake, winding and curving past the most fashionable shops in town. So this is Seville, thought Ellen, the city of tourism, steeped in history and contrast. There were crowded souvenir shops displaying their gaudy wares, and elegant jewelry stores whose gems glistened in the windows and challenged the bright Andalusian sun with their brilliance. It was Seville, city of torrid summers, with tarpaulin-covered sidewalks giving little protection against the high temperatures that made siestas a necessity rather than a pastime.

Again the image of Sandy flooded her thoughts. Sandy, who could have shared all this with her now. But no, that could not be possible at all. She knew that she had allowed herself to lean too hard, sometimes surrendering her own identity to his better judgment, as he had wanted her to do. At times something within her wanted to break free, some inner strength topping her consciousness, saying that it was fully grown, wanting to lean no more. Theirs was not a union of passion; love was more the feeling of comfort and security.

It was too easy, and she had smothered the inner cries, hoping that someday she would combine their relationship with this new awareness of herself. She wondered now if the awareness was buried too deep to summon from the depths where it was placed to bide its time.

Amparo was ahead of her looking in the window of a shop displaying old Andalusian-gypsy costumes and accessories. There had been no one in the *antesala* at breakfast. Louisa did stop in the room briefly to rearrange some platters on the buffet, but all the while she was doing this, Ellen realized that the servant's eyes were on her. Fortunately it was at that point that Amparo dashed into the room and announced she was ready to guide Ellen through the town. The day was bright, and Ellen welcomed the thought of leaving the villa for a short time.

"Señorita, this would look lovely on you for the festival at the villa." Amparo, dancing up and down, broke Ellen's thoughts as she looked in the shop window.

"*Qué bonito el traje.*"

"Amparo, if we are to be partners, you must speak to me in English for a few days longer until all my knowledge of Spanish returns to me. Tell me more about the festival. When will it be held?"

"Oh, señorita, it is a marvelous time when everyone dresses as they did one hundred years ago. They wear mantillas and pretty colored dresses with ruffles." Ellen caught something in Amparo's face that showed some happiness as being a part of her remembered past. At this point she realized that it was yesterday for which they each longed.

"I will wear a red dress." Amparo continued to dance as her eye caught a red flamenco outfit in the window. "What will you wear, Señorita Ellen?"

"I'm not sure that I am expected to dress up."

"Oh, but you are. I know my father will want you to," she said shyly.

Ellen remembered that the child assumed at their first meeting that she was one of Joaquin Pedregal's friends. Thinking back, that was exactly what the doctor thought when they first met. With all this intrigue over Joaquin she was looking forward to meeting this gentleman. As a matter of fact, she felt a little miffed that no one from the family bothered to acknowledge her presence that morning. She was a guest, and it would have shown a little graciousness on the part of Madama Pedregal or Joaquin to greet her last evening or, at least, that morning. As she was beginning to feel pushed aside again, she was aware that Amparo was chattering in the background.

"Let's go talk to him," the child was saying.

"I'm sorry, Amparo. Who should we go to meet?"

"Doctor Bradshaw," she answered. "I do love Doctor Bradshaw."

Ellen's arms went limp at her sides. There was no one she would rather bypass at that moment than Dr. Bradshaw. She had been relieved at the thought of missing him last evening at dinner, though it was obvious they would be seated at the same table before the day ended. But this was too soon. She wanted to be prepared to spar with his sarcasm, and it was too early in the day to have armed herself for anything but pleasant tasks and encounters. She looked down the street and realized he had seen them. It was too late to vanish. Besides, Amparo would only be confused if Ellen refused her their meeting.

As the doctor approached, Amparo left her side and ran to give him a strong embrace around his waist. Then they both walked arm in arm toward where Ellen was standing.

"I didn't know you two were such good friends," she ventured, for lack of anything else to say as an opener.

"Oh, Amparo and I go way back," he said laughingly.

Ellen noticed an air of casualness about him today. He had shed his formal suit and replaced it with an open-collared, print shirt and light blue slacks.

"I didn't realize you had been at the villa that long."

"I haven't been here that long, but I feel as though I've known Amparo all her life," he answered, his smile sobering a little.

What a curious thing to say, thought Ellen. Again she felt that he was trying to tell her something.

"My dear Señorita Amparo." He was bending toward the child. "May I show my happiness over seeing you by offering to treat you to a sweet in the *dulce* shop down the street?"

"Don't you think it's a bit too near lunch, Doctor?" she asked. Though she was not the child's governess, she felt responsible for asking her to town in the first place.

"Come, Miss Ross, give someone else a chance to be gallant other than Señor Joaquin. Amparo will pick out something that she will save for later. Besides, I would like to talk to you."

"Well. . . ." Her curiosity was intrigued. "Only a small sweet to be had after lunch."

Amparo took the change from the doctor and walked down the street to the store, but only after giving the doctor another large embrace.

"She really is fond of you," Ellen said, concerning the child.

"And I am fond of her. But I really want to talk about you, Miss Ross. How have you enjoyed your stay at the villa so far? Let's see, you have been here a little less than twenty-four hours, but I'm sure you've come to some conclusion about your surroundings?" he questioned.

"Are you really concerned about how I've been doing," she asked, "or are you waiting to hear that I'm not faring very well?"

"Now which do you think is true of the two choices you just gave me?" he said, his lips holding back a grin that she was sure would fluster her if he allowed it to break.

"I haven't really begun working yet. I've only glanced at the paintings. The surroundings are too new to me. I'd like to get a feel for the area first. I do feel though—well . . . it's not my business," she stammered.

"No, go on, I'm willing to listen to what you think," he said quietly, his face taking on a very serious expression.

"There's just something . . . unhappy about the villa. The child, for instance, so lonely, so lost."

He did not answer her immediately. There was a sudden silence between them that she had not expected. As a matter of fact, she thought they had been getting on comparatively well, for the two of them.

"Miss Ross, listen carefully to what I say," he finally answered. "Don't get involved here. Do your work and then leave. From what I hear, you are to appraise the Perez paintings for the Pedregals. Involve yourself with the old paintings. Leave the present alone." His eyes were blazing, and after getting over the initial shock of his stinging words, she felt the anger racing through her veins.

"I promise to leave the present alone, Doctor, if you promise to leave me alone. I don't know why you think I'm here—oh, yes, you said I was looking for romance and adventure. Well, I'm sorry to disappoint your stereotyped picture of a young girl in a foreign country, but I happen to be a professional here on assignment. I work very hard in my field, and I take pride in my research and the results of it. I will do my work to the best of my integrity, and if that means dabbling in the present, all well and good. Now if that doesn't suit you, I suggest you continue your own business—whatever that may be—and leave me to mine."

With that, she brushed past him intending to retrieve Amparo from the candy shop and take an alternate street to where Felix would be waiting for them with the carriage.

She was very happy that Amparo was full of chatter and paying no real heed to her as they walked to find Felix. Ellen had to blink very hard to keep the tears that were stinging her eyes from coming in torrents down her cheeks.

Ellen brushed her hair rapidly, having already decided that the dining hour would be unpleasant. She chose a pink dress for the evening, pretending that its color would bring out the pink in her cheeks, but knowing that her flush would be an accumulation of anger and hurt feelings. Dr. Bradshaw had the uncanny ability to release confusion of feelings in her. She disliked him intensely, and yet somehow she wanted him to like her. How ridiculous, she thought, as she tossed her head and almost undid all the work she had just accomplished with her hairbrush. Finishing the last touches, she decided that she would not allow him to interfere too much with her evening. She would pretend he was not even there.

Sherry was to be served in the open-air patio, and as she descended the stairway, she noticed that the others had already assembled.

"Miss Ross, we have been waiting for you." A very tall man with an angular face and very dark, serious eyes approached her. As he came nearer to

her, his step slackened, and she could tell as he
furrowed his brow and stared that he was surprised at the sight of her. He too expected someone older, she thought. But before she could
ponder this any further, he extended his hand to
meet hers.

"I am Joaquin Pedregal. Come, may I present
my mother, and of course, you have met our other
houseguest Eric Bradshaw."

"I've already had the pleasure of meeting Miss
Ross. We shared a carriage ride with Felix from
the station."

"Yes, so you've told me, Eric. And the good
doctor has also told us how happy Amparo appeared in your company today."

"She is a lovely child," Ellen said, throwing a
quick glance at the doctor who was now looking
at the floor as if he felt the embarrassment that
this awkward moment brought her.

"Yes . . . yes . . ." Joaquin seemed as though he
were thinking faster than he was speaking. Finally
he said, "Yes, I do feel that you have brought a
breath of fresh air to the villa, Miss Ross—to
Amparo—and, who knows, perhaps to all of us.
Here, let me get you some sherry."

Ellen was happy at that moment that everyone's eyes left her to follow Joaquin's movements
as he filled a glass of amber sherry for her at the
small bar to the side of the cocktail table.

As Joaquin poured the drink, she raised her
head to look at the starry night above her. At that
moment she picked the brightest star she could
find and wished very hard that she would have

the mental strength to get through the rest of the evening.

"You will be happy during your assignment here, Miss Ross. I am sure of that," Joaquin was saying. "Look at the marvels of this villa. Over two hundred years old, it's a history book in itself."

Ellen looked up at the man as he stood before her waving his arms and throwing accolades at his surroundings. He was handsome and tall, and used every charm of his heritage as he talked of his estate.

"Don't you think Miss Ross will enjoy her stay with us, Mother?" Joaquin continued.

It was a few seconds before the older woman answered, but Ellen knew that the woman had formed a definite opinion of her in those moments.

"I'm sure it will be a pleasant stay," the woman said. Her speech was measured and aloof. "This is a lovely house," she continued, "and every inch of the estate has been with the Pedregals for centuries." She seemed to be speaking more to herself than to her guests.

"Aside from Eric's chalet and the villa, we also have a small *finca*, or ranch, as you would know it. This used to run close to the villa, but Mother had most of the land filled in with gardens when she married my father. There is also some land adjacent to the ranch that is now undeveloped. However it will not be in that state too long. It will soon be developed and added to the estate."

"I should think that the estate is quite impressive as it is," interjected the doctor very quietly.

"Oh, but the bulls have done well for this family for many years. The ranch will even be more magnificent when the additional land is added to it," answered Joaquin.

"Will you continue to be on the road, Joaquin?" asked his mother. "When do you begin participating in the festivals?"

"I must start negotiating for next year's festivals this fall," he said. "You see, Miss Ross, as an impresario, I take the heritage of Spain all over the country to the people. Some of the fairs are held in the most remote areas. There is bullfighting, of course, and we also take with us a troupe of dancers and usually a small group of actors."

"I've heard that in some of the smaller *pueblos,* the people prepare all year for this outing," commented the doctor.

"That is so," answered Joaquin. "In some cases the festival would be the people's only recreation for the entire year."

"Our people work very hard, and Joaquin is a good impresario, a true Pedregal," said Madama. "But we speak too much about ourselves. Miss Ross, tell us something about your life."

Ellen felt herself coloring. She was not prepared for this sudden change in the conversation. Then she quickly reprimanded herself. What was wrong with her since her arrival here—coloring and blushing not unlike an ingenue in her first high school play. If only Dr. Bradshaw were not on the scene. But why should his presence unnerve her so? She was used to meeting all types of people in her work, and her social presence was certainly not lacking—until now, at least.

"I . . . I'm mostly interested in the arts, Madama. I like to spend most of my time in museums or at the theater."

"And, you are alone? No ties, no family?" the old woman queried. "Adventurous sort then, Miss Ross?"

"Ahhem—" the doctor was clearing his throat. "Is that Ana summoning us to dinner?" he asked.

As Ellen's head turned toward the entrance of the patio, she saw one of the servants just turning the corner into view. Either Dr. Bradshaw had an acute sense of hearing, or his timing in saving her from Madama's obvious insinuations was purposeful. Madama's opinion of her was the same as the doctor's then. That she was an adventurer, wandering the earth with no particular ties. But since he thought the same, why did he bother to interrupt and save her feelings that he realized by now would be offended by the old woman's gentle but obvious comment?

"Oh, yes . . . I see Ana is here," answered Joaquin. "Doctor, will you take Mother? I will escort our new guest. Then after dinner, Miss Ross, I will show you some of the beauty of our estate."

After a quick glance at Dr. Bradshaw, she allowed Joaquin to take her arm and lead her from the patio.

CHAPTER 4

To her surprise Ellen spent a delightful dinner hour in the grand dining room. The *sala*, as Madama called it, was stark, with white walls and very little furniture, which was heavy with ornate carvings. In one corner of the room was a small fountain constructed of the same red tile of the patio. At intervals along the walls were placed black iron sconces containing red candles. The upholstery of the dining chairs was red and white brocaded silk.

The sherry that Joaquin had served her had dulled her misgivings for the moment, and she felt inner warmth for the first time since her arrival. It was also the first time that she felt welcomed, and this was due to Joaquin, who spent most of the dining hour doting on her. Madama said nothing at all, and the doctor little more. In fact Ellen felt that Dr. Bradshaw resented the gay chatter between herself and Joaquin and that he seemed to become more sullen as the dinner progressed. This seemed to elate her. She did not know what bothered the doctor, and at that moment she did not even care. The more sullen he appeared, the more effort was made on her part to be charming and interesting in her conversation with the young landowner. This was not difficult, however, as she found Joaquin a gallant and gracious host.

She and Joaquin continued to chatter, and finally the doctor did speak, spattering out his words awkwardly as if his main purpose was to interrupt the easy small talk of the other two young people. "I don't understand why you even want to bother developing your excess land, Joaquin, when you will be traveling with those festivals a lot of the time. Doesn't that place a large burden of responsibility on your shoulders? How can you be in two places at once?" he asked.

"I will not be in two places, Eric. The traveling festivals are well organized, and all are similarly planned. I will still oversee the arrangements, but it would not be difficult to find someone to manage the fairs for me. No, Eric, my place will be here. With a larger ranch, we could even present more activities right on the estate. We already offer one of the best fiestas in the region. That will be coming up soon, Miss Ross, and you and Eric will be able to see what the Pedregals can do," he laughed.

"I'm already aware of the Pedregal charm," Eric Bradshaw said, a bit sarcastically. "And I'm aware that the Pedregals are known to be one of the best families in the region. That's why I think you should redirect and broaden your name in another dimension."

"I don't understand, Eric."

"It's very simple," the doctor said. "You have become too insular in your efforts to spread the Pedregal name even farther than it reaches now.

Do something away from yourself—for the community, for instance. This will give a new dimension to your family—a benevolent one."

"I know what you are getting at, Eric. But we are always present at any benefit that is organized in town. The Pedregals have always participated in these events," answered Joaquin, a bit puzzled.

"Do something bigger," continued Eric Bradshaw.

"What, then?"

"I . . . I don't know," he answered. "Let me think about it, okay?"

"All right, Eric. I am most pleased. Not only do I have a dedicated medical man as a houseguest, but even a part-time public relations man. All well and good. You think of a way to make the Pedregal name even greater than it is. But it will have to be something better than my land development—which will make this the best ranch in the area."

"How about medicine?" continued the doctor, still pursuing the topic. "The medical profession is always in need of funding. That would be a very altruistic gesture on your part and the part of the Pedregal name."

"Yes, and there's the poor and the hungry and the arts and the libraries. I agree, Eric, there is so much that is needed in the south. How does one begin to choose when to be benevolent? But I have the answer to all of it."

"Well, then—what is that?" asked the doctor soberly.

"When this family and our estate is settled and

the new land developed and added to the ranch, I plan to hold a few benefits right here on the estate. In fact you gave me a great idea, Eric. I will hold one benefit a year—each year for a different cause. And, in your honor, the first one will be directed toward medicine. How about that, Eric?"

Why was the doctor pushing him? she asked herself. Why was he so against Joaquin's development of the land? Could Eric Bradshaw be so self-centered and dull that he resented anyone's activities if they fell beyond his sphere of interest?

"Think about it, Eric, how many areas will benefit by our ranch expansion. Now, while you are thinking, I am going to take my leave . . . Mother, with your permission . . . and escort Miss Ross on a tour of this great estate. Come, Miss Ross, I will have Felix prepare the carriage."

When Ellen realized that no one was to go with them on the carriage ride, she almost feigned tiredness as an excuse to withdraw from the outing. Since the last few hours had been delightful, she could not exactly put her finger on the reason for her hesitancy. Perhaps she was afraid that somehow the bubble would burst and she would be back to the state of depression she was in during the train ride through Spain. Or was it that at all? she asked herself. Wasn't it Joaquin himself who was causing the feelings of hesitancy in her? Was she afraid to be alone with him? No, she realized that she did not fear him as much as her own emotions. Her energies were low and this man warm and welcoming. She did not want to

place herself in a lonelier position by allowing
herself any deep feelings for this man. She would
be there for a short time, and then she would
leave that place forever. Yet she was vulnerable
and at this point an easy prey to kindness, especially from such an exciting person as Joaquin.

How absurd all these thoughts seemed as she
rode beside him in the carriage seat. His chatter
was gay and natural as he described the terrain
and named almost every tree and flower they
passed along the road. He seemed very expansive
in his personality and almost naive in his love for
the estate and the area he lived in. He handled
the carriage with finesse, and she assumed his
ranching abilities were as enthusiastic as his
feelings about everything else he spoke about. He
was a great contrast to Eric Bradshaw, she
thought. He had allowed her to enjoy the evening
at least, and for this she was thankful. Her realm
of responsibility had nothing to do with the
money that would be received from the sale of the
paintings once they were authenticated.

"This is where we stop," he said as he finally
pulled on the reins. "It's not far from here. We'll
walk a few paces."

As he helped her down from the carriage, Ellen
felt a bond of closeness to him. She must not do
this, she thought. She must quell her imaginings.
After the loneliness she felt on the train and the
cold antagonism of Dr. Bradshaw, she would
warm to anyone who was pleasant to her. And
that was all that Joaquin was displaying—the
simple kindness and graciousness of a good host.

"Look," he was saying. "You can see the lights of the city from here. Seville is like an old garden left to us by the Moors. But mostly, Miss Ross, its magnificence is the pride of its people that has been handed down from the conquistadores. It is a negative from the past that never faded to remind people of the grace of another day and the dreams that went with it."

"I walked through a part of it today," she answered in a hushed whisper. "I did find the part I saw quite charming."

"And still they continue to build those skyscrapers, away from the earth," he hadn't heard her, but was lost somewhere holding on tightly to another century. "It is unnatural to go away from the earth here because it is from this red earth that we grow our olive trees and to it that we send our cattle to graze. And it is on the red arena that the bullfighter gives his life to prove the courage of his people."

She was overpowered by this man, so engrossed in his eulogy of centuries past. He would have been placed perfectly on a ship for Queen Isabella, sailing around the world adventurously as a loyal subject to his sovereign.

Ellen looked around and saw some scaffolding ahead as they made their way forward through the honeysuckle and jasmine. Perhaps it was the jasmine making her mind sickly sweet and sentimental.

"Come with me a moment, Miss Ross, and I will show you something beautiful." He took her hand and led her to the back of the garden and a platform surrounding a high wall. As they climbed the steps, she could hear odd sounds, like pigs or cows.

"Here señorita, is something as beautiful as a jasmine bough."

As she looked over the wall, Ellen saw a black animal enclosed in a circular fenced area. Startled, she asked, "What is it?"

"It is a bull, señorita. Well, why do you laugh?"

"You said it would be beautiful," she chuckled, and realized it was the first time she had heard her own laughter in a long while.

"But it is beautiful. You have yet to understand the beauty of this animal. Before you leave here you will know the beautiful ones from the ugly, the brave from the cowardly. I will teach you, Ellen. Perhaps I will let you try a few passes with the cape one day."

"Oh, no, to that I must say no," she answered.

He was looking down at her from his towering height, his face tender and a little serious. "You must not be afraid. It is a magnificent experience, all of it—even practicing in the morning hours. Your shoes are wet from the dew on the grass. But it is not really dew. It is a sacred water that baptizes the freshness of the earth at that early hour. It is cool in the morning. Yet behind the hills comes the rose-colored rays of the sun like fingers, taunting, teasing, promising the clearness of the day. And then the bulls . . . you take your cape and start pursuing a few. Aye, even in their savage wildness as they come toward you, and in your own desire to conquer them, you are com-

rades alone in the open space. You could be anywhere at that moment. You can even feel your
own pride and strength running quickly through
your veins. The world around you stops, and
there is only the sway of the cape and the bulls
passing closer and closer. You keep coaxing, passing, and outwitting them. In a while the sun is
higher in the sky and the drops of sweat come
down your face—but you cannot stop. Soon they
are hypnotized by your mastery, and you plunge
for the final taking."

The image was painted; the brush strokes first
erasing the tall, dark figure of the master, and
then drawing in its place the auburn-haired silhouette of Sandy. Their backgrounds were different, but the same drive and illusions were there.

"My ranch is not large enough to fit the image
of what my family stood for in the last centuries.
But soon, soon that will be different," he was saying.

They had both been standing in the direction
of the city lights as he had spoken his dreams.
Now Ellen felt his hand on her left arm as he
turned her to face him.

"Ellen, it is a miracle that you should arrive
here now on this assignment of yours. You will get
to love the estate as I do. I will show you everything. I will teach you everything. Ellen—" She
felt his hand move along the sleeve of her blouse
to her shoulder. Suddenly he cupped his palm at
the back of her neck, and she saw the urgent look
on his face as he pulled her toward him, his lips
showing no mercy as they first moved desperately

over her face and then, finding her mouth, brought an ecstasy to her that she could not and would not control. She was ready then as he pulled her tightly against him and showered her with words she could not understand, but with caresses to which she easily responded.

"Ellen . . . Ellen, it is a good omen that you are here."

"Joaquin . . . I . . ." she stammered.

"I know, I've overwhelmed you," he said abruptly. "Come, I will take you home. Forgive me, Ellen. I am usually more of a gentleman than this, but your presence here will do all of us a lot of good." With that, he took her hand and led her to the carriage.

"On the way home I'm going to teach you a little song that the children sing in the parks as they play," he said as he helped her mount the carriage step.

True to his word, he taught her a playful little Spanish song as the carriage made its way back to the villa. Nothing was said personally between them, which she felt was odd since their explosion of emotions had been so intense for those few moments before. She wondered if he were just trying to cover her possible embarrassment over the incident, or whether he was really able to cut off his feelings as abruptly as he had.

There was a quick bidding of good-night on the patio as he left her to go up to her room alone. She felt incomplete and void. She had feared the effect of Joaquin's graciousness and attractiveness on her weakened emotional state. His advances toward her now seemed a gesture—of what? she thought.

The idea of leaving the country for this assignment had been a solace to her, and she had clung to its idea as a protection against the hurt she had felt over the breakup with Sandy. The idea of leaving the area where she and Sandy had loved soothed her and quieted her. The wound was just beginning to heal, but she was still an innocent traveler in the world of new emotions, with new people. Sandy had been there so long, his ways and feeling so familiar to her, almost predictable without being boring. Now she had to test the water slowly. There should be no brash plunging into the world of caring, of feeling. She would eventually swim and let the waves of emotion strike her body, awakening all the fire and exhilaration that she knew she possessed. She had felt the warmth within her surge to the surface that evening—but was it really for Joaquin? He was an interesting and exciting man—so much like Sandy. No, she would take a deep breath and start over the next day. If the relationship between herself and Joaquin were to grow—all well and good. But now she must concentrate on her assignment and let love fall where it would.

CHAPTER 5

Ellen stretched herself across the bed, slowly opening her eyes to face the new day. She had slept well, and both her body and mind seemed to be at peace. The window was left partly open the night before and now her skin could feel a hint of coolness from the morning air, as if the torrid day were not quite ready to wake. It was the end of the season and the sun's tired rays leaned reluctantly over the earth . . . lazy and spent from the long summer.

She stretched herself again and decided that she would hold on as long as possible to the warm day. After breakfast she would explore the villa and search the library shelves. The Pedregals insisted that somewhere in the house she would find documentation on the authenticity of the Perez paintings. She chuckled to herself as she thought that what the Pedregals really needed was a good detective to find clues that would value the paintings. Of course she would not perform any tests on the artwork before exhausting the search for the documents. She knew she couldn't complain. The Pedregals had made a deal with Jim Bradley that the document search would be part of her assignment. It seemed to mean a lot to the Pedregals to have someone from the United States authenticate the art work.

Ellen reluctantly got out of bed. She was pleased at her own good spirits that morning.

Careful not to rush her ablutions, she sat at the dressing table brushing her hair a full hundred strokes. She was very aware of a ravenous appetite, which she also decided was a good indicator of her feeling of well-being.

The *antesala* was empty as she entered, and this disappointed her. She wanted people there— someone—to notice how well she felt. Then she laughed. People, other people, felt like this every day. But to her, happiness seemed to be a rarity and she demanded an audience when the feeling actually appeared. No matter, she thought. She served herself from the buffet and sat down at the table with a hearty appetite. She was not used to the thick syruplike coffee that was served, but she had indeed become a new fan of *churros*, coiled breads fried in a caldron of burning oil. Amparo had mentioned that *churro* vendors were stationed along the streets in Seville every morning as the cocks crowed and servants from the different households went out at an early hour to purchase the fresh bread for their charges. Ellen was just finishing her second helping of these when Joaquin entered the room. She looked up at him soberly, not sure what his attitude would be toward her. She could not help but notice that he looked quite attractive that morning.

"Ah, Ellen, how lovely you look today," he said charmingly, but with no real personal inflection, she thought.

"Thank you, Joaquin. It's such a lovely morning, I thought I'd take a walk around the estate before beginning the search for the documents," she answered, trying at first with effort to be as casual as he and then finding it no effort at all.

"The estate is yours to do with what you like, Ellen. However, you must promise me one thing."

"And that is . . . ?"

"You will remain as fresh and beautiful as you look this moment and accompany me to the Britz Café for lunch."

"Oh," she laughed, "I thought there was a problem."

"No, not in the least. You are an important guest here, Ellen, remember that. And you must let us know if there is anything you need."

"Everything is fine, Joaquin. I'm perfectly comfortable."

"Very well. Then I'll see you at one o'clock. We'll take the carriage to town."

There was a rustling at the entrance to the *antesala* as Louisa appeared. Both their heads shot up to look at her. Ellen was afraid that the sudden lull in their conversation might have given Louisa the idea that they had been speaking about something clandestine.

"Excuse me," mumbled the girl.

"Louisa, I want you to be sure that Miss Ross has everything she needs while she is staying with us," Joaquin broke in.

"Oh, yes, señor, we have tried to make her comfortable," she answered, throwing Ellen an accusing look.

"That's fine," he said a little impatiently.

"Louisa and the staff have been very kind, Joaquin," Ellen added.

"I'll see you before lunch then," he commented as he left the room.

Louisa's eyes trailed after him and then settled on Ellen.

"You have a lovely dress on today," Louisa said. "Blue is Señor Joaquin's favorite color. You wore it for him then?" she asked.

Ellen blinked a few times as she stared at the housekeeper. Why hadn't she thought of this before? Louisa didn't care that the age of the researcher might affect the accuracy of the tests made on the paintings. But she did care about how the age of the researcher might affect the young landowner.

"I haven't been here long enough to know that the color blue is Señor Pedregal's favorite. Isn't that true, Louisa?" she asked.

"The dress is lovely, señorita," the girl said again sullenly.

"Thank you," Ellen answered, trying to hide her annoyance. She hoped that she would not have to fend off additional jibes of this sort from the girl during her remaining days at the house.

It was even more ironic, thought Ellen, that Louisa should be suspicious of her intentions that particular morning. She was almost sure that she and Joaquin had had their moment—and it would not return again. Oh, he had been gracious and charming in speaking to her a few minutes before, but there was nothing personal in his manner.

And what of last evening? Was lovemaking part of the host's role at the villa?

More surprising to her was the fact that she did not feel particularly upset about Joaquin's casualness that morning. After the first few minutes of speaking to him there was no effort on her part to be just as casual. Then what had the caresses of the previous evening meant to her? It was not in her role as a guest to be accommodating to him. She had felt a fire surge through her—it had been real; it had been intense.

"Señorita." Louisa's voice beckoned her away from her thoughts. "Madama wishes to speak to you. Would you come with me now?"

"Yes, I have just finished breakfast." Luckily, she thought, as Louisa seemed disinterested in the state of her appetite.

She followed the housekeeper across the patio and up the long staircase. Madama's rooms were on the opposite side of the landing from Ellen's, but her door opened into a suite of rooms instead of a single bedroom as Ellen occupied.

Madama was sitting in an easy chair in her small sitting room when Ellen entered. She wore a long dress of dark-green-and-white print and a large emerald brooch was pinned to its collar. She looked the perfect duenna, a role which Ellen surmised was enjoyed thoroughly by the old woman. She was thin and wiry with wrinkled skin on her face and hands. Her black hair was heavily streaked with gray and pulled back to a bun at the nape of her neck.

"Please sit down, Miss Ross." She waved her

hand over to an adjacent chair. Ellen noticed a large emerald ring on her right hand and a number of gold bracelets on her wrist.

"I have brought you here," she continued, "to discuss plans for the coming festival."

"Amparo mentioned something to me about the festival the other day."

"We are holding the festival a little earlier this year—oh, by just a few weeks—so that you may view it."

"But, Madama—" Ellen felt flustered "—there's no need to go through all that trouble. It would, of course, be very enjoyable, but you need not schedule it earlier on my account."

"Nonsense, child. It has already been decided. You must remember, the Pedregals do everything in a grand manner. Look at this villa, Miss Ross. It is a grand villa. The furnishings, the best that could be found in Europe. The tapestries, authentic and elegant. The paintings . . . the paintings . . . all the best."

There it was again, thought Ellen, the element of urgency in both Joaquin and now Madama at the importance of her presence there and the fact that she would be determining the value of the Perez paintings, if they were Perez paintings. It was natural, of course, for anyone to be pleased in having rare paintings in their home. But there was more than just normal pleasure displayed there. It seemed urgent to them that she determine the paintings to be authentic Enrique Perez work. Even Felix had asked her if she would be deciding nice things for the estate and for Joaquin.

"I am very impressed with the estate," Ellen said, "and it's easy to detect with the naked eye the opulence of the villa and the time and patience put into its construction and furnishings."

"Thank you, Miss Ross. And, oh, yes, our dressmaker will be here for fittings at the end of the week. Why don't you take Amparo to the fabric store on Tetuán Street to choose cotton material for each of you." Her words were meticulously enunciated, and her speech was slow and aloof.

"I didn't realize I was supposed to dress."

"But, of course, Miss Ross. Everyone dresses for the festival. It is the grandest event in all of the region. Of course the dress is a gift to you."

Ellen thanked the woman for her benevolence. Yet somewhere in the back of her mind she felt that family tradition was the uppermost thought in the old woman's mind. If this included benevolence, all well and good. But if maintaining the old traditions were to be at the cost of anyone's expense, what then?

"Of course," the woman was continuing, "the estate will be more impressive when Joaquin acquires and develops the additional land to extend the ranch."

"Acquires?" Ellen asked. "Is it not Pedregal land now?"

"Oh, how silly of me. There are a few legal papers to be signed—mere trivialities. The plans for development are almost solidified. It would be grand," she cooed.

Something in the woman's manner showed a

cold shrewdness and interest only in her position as grande dame of the manor.

"This—career of yours, Miss Ross, takes you to many fascinating areas, no doubt?"

"Yes, location assignments are fun," said Ellen.

"And your family, do they not object to your traveling?"

"Oh, I think they are used to it by now. Although not all my assignments are on location."

"And do you live with your family at their home when you are not traveling?"

"No, I've had my own apartment for a few years. When my sister married and I began my work, my parents sold their home."

"Sold their estate?" the woman gasped.

"Well, it was not really an estate," she laughed, "just a small colonial house with an adequate backyard."

"But to sell it. Where do they live now?"

"They have a lovely apartment of their own that is adequate for the two of them. They travel quite a bit themselves and no longer require a house with all the care that is needed for it."

"But, of course, the servants would take the burden off them. . . ."

"Yes, well, Mother always maintained the house on her own. Jed, the gardener, came in once a week."

"Only once a week?"

"Well, Dad liked to putter around the garden, and they only used Jed for the larger tasks."

"My, my. . . ." Madama clucked as she stared incredulously at the young girl. "I imagine you have research to do. I'll tell Amparo that you will take her to town today or tomorrow to pick out fabric then," said the woman with a final note of dismissal.

"Thank you, Madama," answered Ellen, relieved that the interview was over.

The sun was bright, and the flowers surrounding the villa in their garden beds sparkled in its brilliance. Ellen felt the warmth penetrate her skin, and a feeling of relaxation and well-being engulfed her. The interview with Madama had put a slight damper on her early morning exuberance, but she felt that the sun and the beauty of the villa gardens were helping to regain her composure. The older woman did pry, she thought. She also wondered what Madama thought of her family background after she admitted that there had been no array of servants at her family "estate." She laughed at the word after it passed through her mind. No, the little colonial house on Spring Street with its single dogwood tree and hyacinth beds could not be called an estate by any means. Then she chuckled aloud. It was a castle, she thought. But she was sure that Madama would never understand if she had told her that. How could Madama understand that she had lived in a castle when the gardener had come only once a week.

As she reveled between her own private joke and a self-reprimand for being snide at the expense of the haughty woman, her eyes caught sight of the tower standing tall but incongruous to the rest of the house. She decided to walk in that direction and explore the structure before meeting Joaquin for lunch. After lunch she would begin in earnest her search for the documents of the paintings.

As she reached the tower, she noticed that the door was constructed of very thin wood, which did not quite fit its rectangular molding. She pushed it gently, and to her surprise its bolt loosened. The squeaking of the rusty hinge was deafening, and she stopped momentarily to see if anyone was walking about the grounds. Perhaps she should not enter. Yet if this were a place that Joaquin wanted left out of bounds, there would be a better fastening for the door. At most, it could only be a storage area, and Joaquin did tell her to make herself at home.

She pushed the door open and stepped inside. The interior was dark with only the light coming from a slit in the open door giving her any vantage. It was just as she guessed. There were large barrels placed at intervals around the room as well as piles of newspapers, shovels, and ladders strewn everywhere. This was probably a storage area for the workmen of the ranch. She walked around the room sniffing at the mustiness and dodging the cobwebs, which made intricate patterns between some of the farm implements.

As she glanced upward, she noticed that the ceiling was high but not half as tall as the outside structure of the tower. There could be a second landing to the building, she thought. Yet, as she looked around she saw no stairway or lift ladder to reach a second floor. The place intrigued her, and yet she could not determine the reason for her interest. She was about to explore further when she noticed a shadow crossing the open doorway of sunlight.

"Miss Ross, what are you doing in here?" Louisa's voice was ominous, and as she turned to face the housekeeper, she noticed that her face was tense and that she was looking overhead at the ceiling.

"Louisa . . . I was just exploring the grounds before meeting Joaquin for lunch. I'm not planning to begin my work until afternoon." She was annoyed at herself for feeling pressured to explain her actions as a small child would after committing a prank.

"There is nothing for you to see here, Miss Ross. The archives for the art documents are in the library at the main house."

"Louisa, I was certainly not researching here. I told you that I will be beginning my work this afternoon. If I begin this morning, I would only be interrupted by my lunch appointment with Joaquin." This last was said with a sassy tone of which she did not even know she was capable.

Louisa looked suspiciously into her eyes, her face haughty with anger.

"Anyway, Louisa," she sustained her flippancy, "what is so secretive about the tower anyway?"

"There is nothing secretive here, Miss Ross," she answered. "It's . . . there is a lot of debris here—all left by the workmen. We do not wish to be responsible for any accidents."

Louisa's words were so direct that Ellen wondered at first if it could be a warning. Then she quickly dismissed the idea as ridiculous. As she watched the other girl turn and walk out of the tower, she wondered why, through most of her conversation, the housekeeper kept glancing swiftly but urgently up toward the ceiling.

CHAPTER 6

The family custom of riding to town in a horse-drawn vehicle was pleasing to her. Now as she raced down the stone steps to the waiting carriage, she became more pleased at the sight of the young landowner sitting patiently with reins in hand waiting for her to join him.

He offered her his hand, his smile pleasant and natural.

"You did keep your promise, Ellen. You did stay as fresh and beautiful as you looked this morning. How did you spend your time?"

"I . . . walked around the estate. Actually I'm beginning to feel quite guilty of wasting a lot of time since my arrival. I must begin work today."

"Nonsense. As long as you are spending most of that time with me, you have no need to worry." His smile lit his face as his eyes left the drive for a moment to see if she approved of his statement.

"But I really must start this afternoon," she repeated, trying to continue on the more even topic.

"Ah, look, there's Eric," he cut in as he waved his arm.

It was true. They were just out of the main gate and passing the blue stucco house that the doctor occupied. Eric Bradshaw was sitting on the veranda with a newspaper in his hand. He returned Joaquin's acknowledgment with a wave of his own but his face never broke from its somber, disapproving expression.

Ellen had turned her head in his direction but decided not to wave. She was annoyed at him. There was no reason why this man should continue to be antagonistic toward her. They were both guests at the villa, each one with an individual purpose for being there. For some reason he could not grasp the fact that she was there on business, and even if she were there just for a lark, she thought, why would this affect him? He's square, she thought. Grumpy and square. She wouldn't acknowledge him. But he plagued her.

"Has the doctor been here long?" she asked, trying to keep her voice casual.

"He's been here for about a month," Joaquin answered. "A very nice man."

"Is he?" she surprised herself by asking.

"Don't you like Dr. Bradshaw, Ellen?" He laughed.

"Well ... he's ... quite ... sullen."

"Sullen? Oh, I'm surprised to hear you say that. Surprised and happy."

"Happy? Because you agree?"

"No. I just feel that Eric might appear quite attractive to a woman like you. So, I am happy that you dislike him. It gives me a better leeway," he said, a wide grin of satisfaction on his face.

His quips were coming through charmingly, she thought, but a little contrived. Her mind flashed back to the jasmine and the star-studded sky of the previous night. She thought of their closeness of the emotion she felt, and then of the abrupt way that he cooled and taught her the little song on their return home. He remained charming. He was charming that morning in the *sala*. He was being charming now, and flattering, but she felt that his emotion ran no deeper than his facade—his smile, his gestures, his words.

"Aside from that personal aspect," he continued, "I think Eric is nice enough. He is a very dedicated medical man. A serious sort. That might be why you feel he's sullen."

"Is he here on medical assignment?" she ventured, trying to acquire as much information and still remain detached.

"He is doing research on children's blood diseases at various clinics in southern Spain. Poor chap is gone for days at a time because clinics dealing in these diseases are not prevalent here. Often the poor must travel to Madrid and Barcelona for treatment. Of course air fare is prohibitive to some, and even the train fare prevents the trip at times."

"How awful," she answered. "Why isn't a center built here?"

"Ah, Ellen, my benevolent Ellen. That needs funding and interest, both quite difficult to acquire anywhere. But come, let us get on with the happier thoughts. We are about to enter a beautiful area of Seville. It is called the Santa Cruz district and it was a Jewish center during medieval times and remained a fashionable residential area. It should be interesting to you."

The streets in the area were narrow, and

Joaquin quieted as he directed his attention toward maneuvering the carriage, which he did with acute agility.

Ellen noticed that the townhouses were massive, but their bulks were softened by the latticed wrought-iron balconies that acted as trellises to nature's loneliness. Here vines were woven in intricate patterns and were allowed to climb over the facade of the buildings while plants of geraniums, margaritas, and *siemprevivas* were housed in gaily colored pots facing the street and guarding their manors as sentries guarded their palaces years before. The cobbled streets were clean, but there appeared to be a mustiness about, as one would feel in an old museum. The tall buildings, taller than others she had seen in Seville, kept out a lot of the sunlight, and as the carriage neared the edge of the district and Joaquin reined to the left and rounded the corner, a burst of sunlight hit their faces, and she felt that she had just emerged from a theater matinee.

"Did you like it, Ellen? That is what I meant by Seville being a negative from the past. Look over there at the Giralda tower of the cathedral. That same tower was the obelisk of a mosque. The bridge that we see coming into town from San Juan de Aznalfarache was an aqueduct built by the Romans. This is a great city, Ellen, and soon with the development of our adjacent land the Pedregals will be the first family of this area—again in modern times as it was in the past—and you will have helped to make it so."

"I? But, Joaquin, how is that?"

"Well, from the sale of the Enrique Perez paintings, I will develop and expand our estate. And you will have been the catalyst to all of it."

"Joaquin . . ."

"Hush now, and let us hurry. We're already late for our appointment."

She was disappointed that they couldn't return to the conversation about Eric Bradshaw, but the carriage had stopped and after securing the reins, Joaquin took her hand and helped her down to the sidewalk.

The Britz Café was situated directly on the corner of Calle Tetuán and Las Palmas. Its walls sparkled in white marble, and tall French windows dotted its facade. Ellen was stunned at the crowded interior that greeted them as Joaquin led her through the entrance. He was not dismayed at this, as he quickly signaled someone at a table to the far wall, and they continued in that direction.

A short, pleasant man in his sixties stood up as they approached the table. He was dressed entirely in black except for a sparkling white-on-white shirt. A diamond pin held his black tie in place, and a large gold-nugget ring enhanced the little finger of his right hand.

"Don Antonio, our excuses for being late. May I present Señorita Ellen Ross, the art researcher who has arrived from the United States to prepare the papers of authentication on the Enrique Perez paintings."

"Señorita." The man bowed as he took Ellen's hand. "It is so good to meet you." As they seated themselves he continued, "My daughter has wanted the two Perez paintings—with your pardon, Joaquin—since she viewed them three years ago at a gala when Doña Pedregal was still alive. When I learned that they were for sale, I was immediately interested. When will the papers be ready, señorita?" he asked, his eyes flashing in excitement.

Joaquin left her no room to answer. "Don Antonio, I realize your enthusiasm. But you well know the delay of legal documents here in the South. Miss Ross would like to have a stamp of agreement placed on the paintings by her museum, after her recommendation. The mails are slow, and there is the wait of the paper's return from the United States. All in good time, my friend. Miss Ross is going nowhere. She will be here for the great fiesta at the villa and so will you," he laughed, and Ellen thought, a bit nervously.

"With all this double authentication, will the price go up, Joaquin, you rascal?"

"No, everything remains the same, Don Antonio. You have the word of a Pedregal."

"I will leave it to you then. Señorita, I must take my leave now, as I'm already late. I did want to meet you. Joaquin, if not sooner, we will see each other at the fiesta. My personal regards to your good mother." With a handshake to the young landowner and another bow to the girl, he left the table and made his way through the crowded restaurant.

"Joaquin . . ."

"Oh, Ellen, I am thrilled that it will be Don Antonio and his family that will possess the paintings. Don Antonio Vargas is one of the most famous bull breeders in southern Spain. A gentleman, elegant but tasteful. I'm sorry that he had to rush off so soon, but he did want to be presented to you."

"But Joaquin . . ."

"What do you think of this restaurant, Ellen? Do you realize that thousands of dollars of business are contracted here? In the United States large business deals and contracts are negotiated in stuffy law offices. Here most ranch business, bullfighting contracts, and a lot of other deals are negotiated and signed right here in this café. What is it, Ellen?" he snapped. "You are restless."

"Joaquin, the conversation with Don Antonio— he assumes that the paintings are already authenticated."

"Now, my little worrier. We do things differently here. Suppose you let me deal with the people I know in the best way I know. And you, my little dove, just enjoy the surroundings and look over the paintings and prepare yourself to look extraordinary for the fiesta. Come, we will take a carriage ride through the Maria Luisa Park."

"No, Joaquin. I . . . you are being quite gracious escorting me all over town. But I must substantiate to my own employer what I am doing here—and that I am doing something at least."

"You are very conscientious . . . and beautiful. Those two qualities are superb in a woman.

All right, your wish is granted. I'll drop you off at the villa, much against my own desires. But, Ellen, you will begin by looking through my papers for the documents that I know are somewhere at the house. I don't want chemical tests performed on the paintings unless they are absolutely necessary. My father acquired those paintings decades ago and as Mother claims, documents were acquired with them."

"I have no intention of touching the paintings until I've searched extensively for the original documents," she answered.

"Don Antonio is so intent on buying the paintings, Ellen, that all this may not be necessary."

"I don't know what you mean."

"Well, you saw Don Antonio and you heard him speak about the paintings. He cannot wait to get his hands on them. He's even afraid that all this extra work will raise the price. Ellen, you are too conscientious, too formal at times. You can see without question that the paintings are Perez originals. Relax, Ellen. Enjoy your surroundings. Enjoy me . . . and let me enjoy you . . . the way I want to. Let me make you happy, Ellen, let me show you my land, and let me . . . make you happy . . . the way you know I can."

He was looking straight at her now, and his hand had reached across the table to cover hers. She mustered all of her energies to stop herself from pulling away abruptly.

He was charming, she thought, his angular, sensitive face somber now, promising. And he was bribing her.

"Joaquin, I need the light if I'm to get any work done today. And if I'm to stay and enjoy the festival I must sent a report of my progress to Jim Bradley. I wouldn't want him to think that I've been lax in my duties. I don't want to be replaced, you see."

"Replaced? I would not have you replaced."

"Let's go then, Joaquin."

"But we haven't even lunched," he answered, pouting.

"I'll get something at the villa. We must go, Joaquin."

"Very well, very well," he sighed. "I will drive you back. I do have to assemble the men and coordinate their duties in preparation for the festival. But I leave you reluctantly, Ellen, you know that."

"Of course, Joaquin," she answered quietly.

Eric Bradshaw looked up abruptly when Ellen entered the library. He was sitting at the large mahogany desk. The two deep side drawers of the desk were open, and Ellen could see a mass of papers on the desk's surface.

It was evident to each of them that neither one had expected to see the other, and now they froze. Ellen noticed a slight coloration in his face, but other than this he seemed to maintain his composure. Their eyes met, held briefly, seriously, and then he looked down at the papers and proceeded to gather them together as if he were through with them.

"Miss Ross," he broke the silence, his voice lowered, but remained steady. "I thought you were spending the day with Joaquin."

"I'm sure you did," she answered cryptically.

His eyes shot up at her again, his face looked stern for a moment, and then his mouth broke into a wide grin. The grin is what disarmed her most, she thought. If he would just not grin.

"Did you enjoy your ride?" he asked as he sat back in the desk chair as if settling to have a chat with her.

"It was pleasant enough, but the time has come to get down to work—although it seems you have already begun that task for me," she said, indicating the pile of papers with a gesture of her chin.

Looking down at the desk he said, "I . . . was looking for a calendar. I have to plot out a few more trips before I leave here."

Suddenly the thought of his leaving, whenever in the future it might be, angered her. She became very flippant. "What is wrong with the calendar on the desk then, Doctor?"

He looked up at the large gold clock-calendar in front of him and then back at her. "I doubt if the bulk of that one would look very appealing in my hip pocket," he stabbed. "I was looking for a pocket calendar that I might use on my travels."

"Did you find what you were looking for then?" she asked, more angry than before, as she colored from embarrassment.

He was smiling openly at her now, thoroughly

enjoying the predicament he had put himself into, she thought.

"No, I didn't," he answered.

Why did she hate him so? she continued thinking. Why did his smile throw her off her stride? Why did he look at her like that—so candidly, so dissectingly?

"Well, I hope I find what I'm looking for," she sighed. "I really don't know if all this is necessary."

"What do you mean?"

"It seems to me that if extra funds are needed to develop land, Madama could sell half of the baubles on her right hand and save the paintings to boot."

"You're being very cryptic," he said, still staring at her, almost studying her.

"I'm being honest," she said. "Something that you're not doing, Doctor."

"I?" he laughed. "How did I suddenly get mixed up in the search for the documents or the authenticity of the paintings?"

"I'm asking myself the same question," she said.

"I'm here to . . ."

"Oh, yes, I'm sure your visits to the clinics are genuine on your part . . ."

"You've been asking about me then?"

". . . since you are supposed to be a dedicated medical man."

"Have you?"

"Have I what?" she almost shrieked. She did not recognize herself—the tone she was using, the accusations. She prayed she was dreaming all this.

"Have you been asking about me?" His voice had lowered, softer, gentler.

"Just curiosity," she flipped out the words over her shoulder as she walked over to the bookcases.

"I'm sorry then," he said.

"For what?" She looked back at him, sitting on the edge of the desk.

"I'm sorry that it's just curiosity."

"What else would it be?" She had not meant to ask that.

"And how am I being dishonest?" he asked, disregarding what she hoped he would.

"You're also here for some other reason."

"Now how do you arrive at that?" he asked, and this time she noticed that the smile was gone and that his expression became more worried than serious.

"Obvious, that's all."

"Obvious?" He rose from the desk's edge.

"Well, for instance . . . what were you looking for in that desk?"

"A calendar."

"And why are you so afraid of me?"

"Afraid of you?"

"Of my presence here?"

He quieted, taking a long time now to look at her, her face, her hair, down the length of her body—through to the depth of her being, she thought.

"Maybe you're right, Miss Ross. Maybe I am a little afraid of you," he said. Then he threw her another brief grin and walked out of the room.

She forced herself to cast him from her

thoughts, as she busied herself looking through the various documents in the library for the rest of the afternoon. Even at dinner, which that evening everyone took in their own rooms, she was able to keep her focus on what she planned to do the next day.

It was later, as she prepared for bed, that she allowed her thoughts to wander to her conversation with Eric Bradshaw that afternoon. As she thought of him, she felt a sudden loneliness engulf her. Suddenly the air in her room became heavy as if the flowers in her coverlet and draperies were taking all the oxygen that the room offered.

She walked to the window, opened it, and then leaned on the sill to look far across the *campo*. The stars were bright, making patterns over the sky like one of El Greco's paintings that she had once seen at the Metropolitan in New York. The mountains finished the picture rimming the sky in the background, and the moon cast an eerie light, reflecting on the tinsel-colored leaves of the olive trees. Could those branches, moving slightly in the night breeze, lull her into some hypnotic sleep so that she could forget she had undertaken this assignment at all? And the mountains, devoid of heart and soul, looked as if they were shrouded in a shawl of mist even on this starry night. They lamented for her, she thought. If she could run to those hills now and bury herself in their crevices to be devoured while she cried!

She was alone, and she longed desperately for yesterday. And continuing to long for it, she slept.

CHAPTER 7

The grounds of the villa were bustling that morning. Workmen were hauling yards of red-and-white canvas and plank boards to the area far to the left of the tower. There were long tables, chairs, and lanterns strewn in abundant carelessness over the grass and red earth making everything look like the maneuverings of a carnival setting up its facilities for a week of circus performing.

She was waiting for Amparo; they were to be driven to town by Felix so that they might choose fabric for their festival dresses. After viewing the sudden activity in preparation for the fair she was thankful that they had not postponed their duty any longer, although Amparo assured her that Señora Cintron would have the dresses finished in a day or two.

She was a little embarrassed at the declaration of Madama that the festival was being scheduled earlier for her benefit. Another bribe, she wondered? After Joaquin's overtures to her in the café she was a little wary of any niceties. Some of these should wear off on the doctor, she thought, and then purposefully dismissed him from her mind.

She had a lot of work to do, and the trip to town with Amparo had to be short. She had not found any documents in the library desk pertaining to the paintings, though she had yet to search the record books that were contained by the library shelves. This she would do after the trip to town.

She was just beginning to wonder what the estate grounds would look like after the men finished their work, when she heard someone approaching her. Thinking it was Amparo, she turned, only to find Louisa standing behind her, eyeing her fully as she usually did.

"Louisa, how are you this morning?" she asked, trying to be pleasant.

"I am well, Miss Ross. And you, have you been working very hard on the documentation?"

"Yes, but to no avail," she answered, wondering how much family business this girl was in on and then realizing that Louisa probably missed nothing.

"Where will you be working today, señorita?"

"I'll still be in the library." She wondered why the girl was keeping track of her movements. "I've only sifted through the desk papers. I haven't begun to look at the records in the library shelves."

"Señor Pedregal asked me to tell you that I could be of help to you if you need assistance in searching."

"Yes, Louisa, that would be very nice. At the moment I'm going along at a steady, but slow, speed. There are these interruptions though. The family is being so . . . gracious. I am to go with Amparo now to choose fabric for our festival dresses."

"Yes, that is why I have come to speak to you. Madama wishes you to do her a favor."

"Of course. How can I be of service to her?"

"It seems that Amparo has decided on some outlandish colors for her festival dress. Madama wishes you to subdue her taste and see that she chooses something in color appropriate for a child. Would you see to that, Miss Ross?"

"Of course," she answered, taking the request more like a command.

She tried not to show her annoyance, but as she thought about it, she was angry for Amparo. No one from the estate seemed to give much attention to the child. She was pleased to be with Amparo, and she knew that Amparo had taken a liking to her. Yet, it was very inconsiderate of Madama and Louisa not to take time in planning what Amparo should wear for the festival.

"Remember, Miss Ross," Louisa continued. "I would be more than happy to help you search for the documents, if you need me."

"I'll remember that, Louisa," she answered. "Oh, but there is something you could help me with."

"And that is, señorita?"

"That tower. I couldn't help wondering when I was there the other day. The room on the main floor has such a low ceiling in comparison to the height of the overall structure. I cannot imagine someone like Joaquin wasting any available space on the estate."

"The structure intrigues you then, señorita?"

"Only, as I said, in the aspect of wasted space. Of course, there could be another room on top . . ."

"Why did you say that?" the other girl snapped.

". . . but as I was about to say, there is no access to the upper floor."

"Exactly, because there is no upper room," Louisa answered, suddenly calmed by the logical deduction. "There is nothing intriguing about the tower, señorita. Therefore, I would not waste my time doting on it," she said as she turned to take her leave. "Felix should be waiting in front of the house," she added, but she did not tarry to give Ellen an opportunity to walk back with her.

What a strange girl, she thought. And then she checked herself. She wondered at her own reactions to all of these people. She was complicating her life more by becoming involved with their personalities. If she could just do her work, go up to her room for meals, and return to her work again, she would be fine. But life was not like that. She could not live in a vacuum. She thought of Jim Bradley then, and what he would say to all this. *Dear Jim,* she quoted a letter in her mind, *I can't get my work done because I'm too busy being a friend to a lost child. And when I'm not doing that, I'm too busy thinking about why Eric Bradshaw is so negative, Madama Pedregal so pompous, and Louisa, the housekeeper, so mysterious. Oh, yes, and Jim, I'm being bribed by Joaquin. He feels that Don Antonio would buy the paintings in two minutes and that all my research and tests on the paintings, if it comes to testing, are not necessary. He feels that I could see that the paintings are original Perez without*

*going through all that trouble. He feels I should
spend my time with him, having him make me
happy. Oh, Jim, get me away from here. Why did
I come here to forget Sandy? Sandy. . . .* She
quieted in her mental ramblings. Sandy seemed so
far away suddenly. Not forgotten, no, Sandy
would never be forgotten. She loved Sandy as she
did her sister and her parents. But the longing for
him had gone—the longing and passion had never
really been there. Only a security, a steadiness.
When she cried the night before, it hadn't been
for Sandy, but for a life that was all in place. She
would have that again, she willed. But she was
just beginning, and it was natural to feel shaky
when first going out on your own.

She thought of Joaquin then. He was not really
like Sandy, though his ambitious nature was similar. Her feelings for him that evening in the
garden were suddenly apparent to her now. She
had reached for him quickly, wanting no gap between the security of Sandy and the hazy future.
She had passion deep within her—dormant there
with Sandy, but ready, always ready to emerge
and come alive. Joaquin was a link to the past
that evening. She was still holding on, afraid to
let go. And yet her break with Sandy took place
because she could not stifle her mind and her
feelings any longer. She had longed to be free and
to seek life on her own level and be a whole person unto herself. She had to be loved in that way
for all her faults and weaknesses. She would not
compromise. Joaquin was promising her happiness—if she would authenticate the paintings

without further research. She would not do that. Louisa told her not to dote on the tower. She would not do that either. There was something wrong with the tower—something that needed searching into—and she would get to the bottom of it.

She felt so much lighter as she walked to the front of the villa where Felix and Amparo were waiting in the carriage. She smiled at the two of them, and because she was content within herself, she felt that they were smiling at her in an extra special way, though she realized that they could not possibly know the transformation of thought that had just taken place within her.

"Ellen, I'm so excited about choosing the fabric," Amparo exploded, as Felix helped her mount the vehicle.

"I'm looking forward to the ride myself," she confessed.

"Last year I wanted a scarlet dress, but my grandmother said I couldn't have one," the child continued. "I want what I wanted last year," she pouted.

Remembering the burden that Madama had placed upon her, she pondered on how to get the child to change her mind about the outlandish color for the festival dress. Then, she thought of something, and it turned out to have nothing to do with Madama and what Madama wanted.

"I have a marvelous idea," she said to the child. "I think we should celebrate the fact that we have met each other. And, in doing so, Amparo, I think we should embark on something new and forget our yesterdays."

"I don't know what you mean," pouted the child, acting as if she were about to miss something entitled to her.

"This is my very first festival, Amparo, and I am pleased that I will be sharing it with you. I'd like to feel that we are doing something unique together—without having it be something linked to another time—when I wasn't here to share it with you, you see. I think we should choose lovely colors for our dresses, new colors that we decide upon now, together."

"I understand what you mean, Ellen," said the child, "but I wouldn't know which color to choose."

"I know, how about dressing as our favorite flower."

"Oh, no, we couldn't do that," the child answered. "We must wear the traditional flamenco dress of the area, with ruffles and flounces," she pouted.

"I know that, Amparo. But what if we dress in the color of our favorite flower."

The child thought a moment, and then said, "Well, I do love the pink clover. I love the perfume that comes from it."

"Very well, then, Amparo, what about a pink dress, then?"

"Oh, that would be pretty," cooed the child. "With white polka dots?" she added.

"A pink dress with white polka dots, Amparo. That does sound lovely."

"And what about you, señorita?" The child was becoming excited about the game they were playing.

"I think since I've been here I have become very fond of the jasmine."

"Then you shall wear a white dress, Ellen. Oh, I do think this is fun. I know my mother in heaven would approve," she said soberly.

"I'm sure she would, Amparo."

"I wonder if she likes that heaven better," pondered the child.

"Better than . . . ?" Ellen asked, trying not to open a whole new area of conversation that would be sad to the child.

"Better than the one she loved while she was . . . while she was here. It was lovely, her heaven. Once in a while she used to take me to it. It was decorated so beautifully. I used to love to go. But, then she got sick, and I didn't go for a long time, I wish I could find it now—to show you, Ellen."

"You don't know where this place was that she brought you to, Amparo?"

"I've tried to find it many times. I remember it being up very high—at the top of the trees, near the clouds. It was very beautiful."

"Well, you are going to be beautiful for the festival, Amparo. I'm very happy that we've decided on our colors together," she said, trying to change the subject.

The carriage was nearing the outskirts of the city, and Ellen asked Amparo to point out various landmarks to her as they continued the drive. She could not help thinking about Amparo's description of her mother's beautiful room. How strange that the child could not remember where the room was located. Yet, in her mind, she was sure Amparo knew its location.

The trip to town for the dress material was pleasant. Amparo was so delighted at having some attention directed toward her that she insisted on showing Ellen a few sights within the city. This time gnawed into the lunch hour, and they decided to eat in Seville at a small restaurant off Calle Sierpes that Felix recommended. The child ate heartily, and Ellen felt that the time was well spent.

Felix seemed so delighted that Amparo was spending a pleasant day that he insisted on driving through Maria Luisa Park on the trip home. They stopped at varied intervals to enjoy the palms, watch the fountains spout their water and run among the doves and pigeons that abundantly inhabited the grounds.

All of these pleasant activities lingered into the afternoon, and when the carriage finally pulled up in front of the villa, she was again disgusted with herself that she had accomplished so little in her research that day. At first she thought of abandoning the remainder of the day entirely and beginning anew the next morning, but her conscientious nature would not permit that. She decided to venture down to the library to begin searching the shelves for the important documents.

As she left her room for the library, she turned toward her own door to secure its closing, and her eyes happened to linger on a large painting attached to the wall to the right of her door and practically at the end of the landing. The composition, a pleasant, but nondescript landscape, did not catch her attention as much as the way the canvas balanced crookedly from its hanging fixture. She was not one who walked about people's living rooms straightening their art work, but this picture was so large that it looked especially comical tipped in that fashion.

The shock that came over her as the wall panel slid open was indefinable. She had only moved the painting a few inches to the left when she heard the click, and then it had happened. At first she froze, and then it seemed urgent that she look down the other end of the landing and over the railing to the patio to be sure that no one else had seen this extraordinary occurrence.

After she was sure that she was the only witness to the rare happening, she reached over and twisted the painting in the direction opposite to what she had done the first time. She watched, mesmerized, as the panel slowly closed again.

Absolutely entranced by her discovery, she did this entire process another time to be sure that the first occurrence wasn't just a freak happening. Now she peeked behind the open panel and noticed a brass button that would be situated directly behind the hanging fixture of the painting. She pushed the button and ran quickly to the outside landing as she watched the panel close over again. She had found the mechanism to control the panel from the inside chamber of the passage. Now she was ready to proceed.

She moved the painting once more to the left, and again the panel opened. This time she stepped inside of the chamber and quickly pushed the brass button to close the passage behind her. It was done.

It was only then that she realized she had not thought of a means of lighting her way once she was behind the wall.

Her peril was not so great, however, as she noticed narrow slits of windows at random along the high walls of her enclosure. These in turn gave light on what seemed to be a spiral staircase that appeared to go up to the heavens.

As she began to climb, she realized that she was indeed on the upper level of the silo. There had been no access to the upper floor from the storage area because the access was available only from the landing near her room.

The steps seemed inexhaustible, but as she raised her head, she saw that they would terminate at a landing that stopped abruptly at a small wooden door. Would the door be open? She had to see what was beyond that door.

Her surprise was short lived as she entered the room. Hadn't she expected all that she saw? The walls of the room were painted eggshell blue and blended exactly with the blue carpeting on the floor. The four-poster bed contained a coverlet and canopy of a deeper blue field with minute bouquets of tiny white flowers. The dresser had a similar material for its dust ruffle. The most extraordinary feature in the room, however, was the ceiling of octagonal paneled mirrors tapering to a point at the center. It was obvious that this was the top of the tower. This was Amparo's heaven above the trees. This had been her mother's tower in the sky.

Ellen's eyes moved quietly around the room and rested on a rather contemporary floral painting on the wall near an elegant chaise longue. Her eyes rested on it a long moment and then quickly went around to the rest of the room.

The furniture was immaculately clean, and the carpet had been recently vacuumed. She wondered if that was the reason why Louisa had asked where she would be working that day. Louisa was probably planning to clean the tower room and wanted to be sure that no one would be about to ask questions. She might have been in such haste that she left the painting hanging crookedly after she left the chamber.

She felt an urgency now to leave the tower before anyone knew she had found it. What a beautiful hideaway for Amparo's mother, she thought as she descended the spiral staircase. She wondered why the woman used the room. To reflect over happy events, to daydream over happy events that would never come to pass?

As she approached the brass button on the sliding wall, she stopped for a moment, wondering who she would encounter as she opened the door.

She slid out quickly, thankful that no one was in sight. As she entered her room, she was also thankful that dinner would again be served in the rooms that evening. After her discovery she felt that she could not face the others at that time. She thought again of Jim Bradley. "Jim"—this time she spoke aloud—"I'm getting in deeper, Jim. What will be next?" She could not help but spend the rest of the evening reflecting over the beautiful room in the tower and what connection it had on the events of the last few days.

CHAPTER 8

The tower cast a long shadow over the grounds,
but she forced herself not to look directly at it
when she left the villa for a quick morning walk.
No one had been in the *antesala* for breakfast,
and since she knew she must spend the rest of the
day in the library, she felt the urgency of leaving
the house even for a short time. Louisa had met
her as she was about to leave the villa to say that
the family would be gathering for cocktails in the
patio that evening followed by dinner in the *sala*.
Ellen wondered if Eric Bradshaw would also be
there.

She had passed the tower now and decided to
walk in the direction of the corals. She was
tempted to turn and throw a quick glance at the
tall silo, but held her impulse. Louisa might be
watching from a window, she thought. Louisa always seemed to be watching her. She knew that
the girl was completely infatuated with Joaquin.
Or was she protecting the room in the tower from
discovery? It was such a beautiful room, she wondered then why the family wouldn't be proud to
display it.

As she turned in the direction of the corals, she
saw that the area was screened by large bushes
and trees. She thought quickly of Madama and

knew that this attempt at hiding the less aesthetic part of the estate was probably her doing.

She was not completely through the hedge of greenery when she noticed that it opened to face a small bullring.

A man leaned over the brim of the ring, his work clothes starched and clean, allowing him the appearance of a bent scarecrow left over from last year's harvest, though better dressed. Two other figures showed conspicuously in the center of the ring, reminding Ellen of one of Goya's sketches of a man-and-beast tableau. And it could have been a sketch that she viewed, for neither matador nor bull displayed any movement except for an invisible electricity that seemed to pass between their souls.

Joaquin was dressed in the traditional brown Cordobés outfit. The short, waist-length jacket, tight-fitting pants, and flat Cordobés hat with a wide brim made him more attractive than she had ever seen him look. He had been holding two sticks in his hands, their hooked ends shining ominously in the sunlight. Brightly colored paper frills, like gypsy decor, were attached to the ends of the sticks.

Joaquin raised them now, high above his head. He suddenly placed his weight forward on his toes, and with a loud cry he began to prance majestically around the ring as if beginning some ritual of devil worship. The bull kept his body still but turned his eyes slightly to follow the movement of the man, and the title of master still hung in abeyance.

With a sudden turn and another cry—almost as if to warn the bull—Joaquin moved quickly toward the animal and, swaying his steps and body for confusion, ran past the bull, and in doing so placed the two banderillas into the animal's back muscle.

The bull snorted, stamped, and tried to dislodge the uncomfortable pins from his shoulders. They stuck. Joaquin, already at the barrier, was retrieving two more banderillas, and the procedure was repeated in much the same fashion, except that the bull's head hung lower now with the further aggravation of his muscle.

"Give me the muleta," Joaquin was shouting to the workman, but his eyes kept a steady vigilance on the animal, who in turn was scuffing and stamping the earth.

The workman handed the small red cape and sword to the matador and then hovered against the side of the barrier while Joaquin called again to the bull.

This time Joaquin's body was bent backwards, mocking, taunting, and daring the animal to advance. As if by cue, both figures lunged toward each other, the bull missing the man by centimeters while the red cape passed closely over the animal's back.

Again and again the two lunged forward, creating a mystifying hypnotic dance, testing each other's nerve, constantly trying each other's courage and strength. To Ellen's horror this last pass of the cape was too close, and Joaquin was thrown to the ground. All she could see was the

claret blood that covered the right side of his suit.
She stifled a cry—the panic within her paralyzed
her from running to him immediately. Instead she
hid farther into the shrubbery, relieved that the
workman's reflexes were more spontaneous than
her own. The man did run quickly to Joaquin,
who waved frantically at the bull in order to dis-
tract him away from the man.

"Get back," shouted Joaquin, scrambling quite
agilely to his feet. "You fool," he continued. "You
know you are not to interfere while I have the
muleta."

"But, señor . . . you are bleeding . . ." the
workman stammered.

"I am not. It is the bull's blood pouring down
its side from the banderillos. We passed so close
that it rubbed off. You have ruined the feeling between us." With that, Joaquin's hand swung hard
at the man's cheek.

Ellen gasped again, both hands covering her
mouth. She could not believe the change in character occurring in Joaquin since their first meeting. And then, as she thought further, perhaps
there had been no change at all. Hadn't she
sketched her own lord of the manor those first few
hours, depicting him as strong and benevolent
and warm as she needed? Could this cold pompous man be the same one who welcomed her
that evening on the patio of the villa? Or was that
a character in some untitled play that Joaquin
had mentally written for himself, taking on the
role as the gallant rancher, charming and kind?
And she, the audience, had applauded him

silently, encouraging him in his role to suit her own needs. And Madama, the other important character in the *comedia*, wanting more, always more, and sacrificing valuable paintings—perhaps they were valuable—to hold tightly to the image of grandeur, mummified to aristocracy while surrounded by her baubles and servants and land.

Suddenly there was movement behind her, and the whisper—although hardly audible—broke so loudly into her thoughts that she jumped backward from her station behind the shrubbery. She was relieved to see Felix looking bent and very solemn standing near her. She wondered how long he had been there watching her spying on his master.

"Felix, you did startle me." She tried to demonstrate some composure as if eavesdropping on the lord of the manor was something one did every day.

"You are shocked at Joaquin's fervor," he said, as if he cared nothing about her clandestine position.

"The workman was only trying to help him," she blurted out. "The bull did throw him."

"When the señor is in the ring, he will not tolerate interference, especially when he is using the muleta. The great Dominguin was always alone in the ring when it was time for the muleta."

"But, Dominguin. Even I have heard of his mastery with the bulls. Does Joaquin compare himself with Dominguin?"

"He is his idol, we might say. Don't forget,

señorita, Joaquin has great pressure on him to live up to what the Pedregal name demands."

"Or what Madama demands?" insisted Ellen.

"Madama is a proud duenna, and she is on in years. She wants the house restored to what it was in the past. And she wants this done before her death."

"And Joaquin? Is his drive as great for the estate?" she asked.

"Joaquin had potential to become a great matador. Unfortunately, with his father's death, he had to abandon his career. But, I will say yes, his drive is as great for the estate, perhaps even greater."

She had not been wrong then in her reflections. It would be sad enough if only Madama were pushing him to complete her imagery of what role the don should play. But it was Joaquin himself, driving so hard to fit the role.

"He seems to have finished his practice," she said. "The workmen are taking away the bull. I must speak to him."

"How is my little Amparo, Miss Ross?" Felix broke in. "I think she enjoyed the afternoon yesterday very much," he smiled.

"And you helped her enjoy it, Felix. She loved the ride in the park and the restaurant you suggested."

"The time you spend with her, Miss Ross, is more valuable than any decision on the paintings. Do not fret that you have been distracted from your work."

She looked at him, stunned at his wiseness, appreciative of his compliment.

"You are very fond of the family, aren't you?"

"Yes, I have been on the estate a long time—long enough to know that your presence here is an asset, especially to Amparo."

"Thank you, Felix, you're a very kind man to say so."

He nodded, and she watched him step away behind the shrubs in the direction of the tower.

Ellen stood a moment gathering courage to approach Joaquin, who was now taking a drink from an earthen *búcaro* and spitting the water to the sand. It would have to be now, she thought. He did not always appear at dinner, and she wouldn't discuss important matters openly in front of the others even if he were to attend that evening. It seemed as though he kept some separate life for the evenings and disappeared into a private world of his own after dusk. She pulled herself together and stepped away from the bushes.

"Joaquin, I'm pleased to find you. I realize the festival is keeping everyone busy."

"Señorita . . . how long have you been standing there?"

"I just came from the house," she answered, knowing that he would not have wanted her to have seen him be knocked to the ground by the bull nor see his lack of benevolence to the workman. She tried to keep her voice light.

He was looking at her suspiciously, his eyes deep with concern. Then, as if casting off his first disturbing thoughts, his face broke into a smile as he said, "Well, it is good to have a visit from you so early in the morning. It will give me a good start to the day, Ellen. Come, would you like to try a few passes with the cape? I will teach you."

"No, oh, no, Joaquin. I'm not agile nor brave enough to attempt anything like that. I did want to tell you that I'll be spending the entire day in the library looking through the shelf records for the documents. I've found nothing so far, and I've been wondering . . ."

"Wondering what, Ellen?" he said, still smiling.

"Would there be another place, another room that might house these documents?"

"No, I doubt it. All of the family papers are in the library," he answered.

"What about the bedrooms? Could there be important papers in one of the bedrooms?" She was trying him to see if he would mention the tower room.

"No. . . . There are no papers at all in the bedrooms."

"I wonder, then, Joaquin, if we shouldn't just go ahead and begin testing the canvas and the pigments. It would be so much faster, and you could finalize your business with Don Antonio."

"Now, Ellen, why the rush? You are staying for the festival anyway. Keep searching for the documents, and if nothing turns up after you've exhausted the library shelves, then after the festival you can begin working directly on the paintings. I really would like you to handle it that way," he added a little more soberly.

She thought a moment, was about to protest, but changed her mind. She was only an agent of the museum with which the Pedregal family contracted the research and appraisal. In normal circumstances she would not think of protesting against her assignment once she accepted it. But here at the villa she had become so involved with all of the personalities—she almost felt as if she were invited to become involved—that at times she forgot her place and almost became too familiar with the family owning the artwork. They knew what they wanted accomplished and how they wanted it accomplished. What she had to keep in mind was the need to display as much integrity and conscientiousness in her work as possible. If Joaquin wanted her to spend endless hours looking through estate records, then that is what she would do since that was what he contracted with Jim Bradley and the museum.

"I'll be off, then, Joaquin. I'd like to get in a full day of work."

"Will we be seeing you at dinner?" he asked.

"Of course," she answered lightly. "And at cocktails before."

As she turned and walked toward the house, she could feel his gaze upon her. Was he beginning to mistrust her? she asked herself. Had Louisa told him that she was asking questions about the tower? Or was he becoming more tense about the outcome of the appraisal of the paintings?

She was relieved then as she entered the villa

that she would be working alone—away from the others—for the rest of the day.

The dress had a low, V-shaped neckline that edged a rather snug bodice. The skirt was softly flared and reached her midcalf. Not too dressy, she mused as she looked in the mirror, but dressy enough. The rust, brown, and pale orange Chinese figures were good contrast against the white background of the fabric, and as she checked her hair one more time, she felt that she was ready to go down to the patio.

There was a certain excitement about her at the thought of going down to dinner that she could not understand. That's what comes of eating in your room for two nights and spending hours over musty library shelves, she told herself.

She purposefully planned her schedule so that she would arrive early in the open garden. She wanted some time to sit there alone, perhaps sip a sherry, look up at the stars, listen to the trickle of fountain water and just relax. Although this was her intent, she felt no disappointment as she made her way down the staircase and saw Eric Bradshaw already on the patio, mixing himself a drink at the bar. Her pulse seemed to quicken as she made her way into the garden area, and she wondered if she had planned an early arrival hoping for just this situation.

Her face was beginning to flush, but then she checked herself as she remembered that her last meeting with the doctor had not been too friendly. None of their meetings had ever been friendly, she thought.

"Miss Ross," he said as he noticed her. For some reason she felt that his face showed appreciation over how she looked.

"Dr. Bradshaw," she nodded. "We seem to have arrived early."

"I . . . think . . . that it's all kind of nice."

"What is?"

"The fact that we could have a drink together for a change."

"Oh?"

"You don't agree then?"

"Of course. The patio is pleasant. I really haven't had a chance to enjoy it," she said coolly.

He was looking at her intently. His face was quite serious. She sat in a comfortable wicker chair, folded her hands on her lap, and then looked straight up at him, a look of defiance on her face as if daring him to be antagonistic.

"How about a drink? Sherry?" he asked quietly.

"No, I'll take whiskey with water."

"Not your usual drink," he commented.

Now he had been keeping tabs on her, she mused.

"Not so," she answered gently. "You have only seen me drinking sherry. Remember, Doctor, you don't know me very well."

"Oh, I think I do, Miss Ross."

"No. You've just predetermined who and what I am and why I'm here. But you aren't necessarily correct in what you think." She was enjoying this thoroughly, although he looked rather uncomfortable that she had begun the conversation on a note of attack. Good for him, she thought. Let him feel the brunt of someone else's coolness.

"How are you doing in your work?" He turned the conversation as he brought her the drink.

"I'm still searching for the documents," she sighed. "I imagine I'll be working directly on the canvases soon. Nothing has turned up."

"Nothing?" he asked.

"Well, no. I wouldn't be tarrying at the library shelves if I had come up with something."

"I guess . . . all those papers you're looking through are . . . quite interesting. I mean you would have to scrutinize each one pretty carefully if you're trying to find specific documents. Any of them particularly catch your eye?" he asked, looking down at his drink.

"Not really. I do wish I could come up with the . . ."

He looked up at her now. "What's wrong?"

"Why did you ask that? If one of the papers particularly caught my eye?"

"No reason." He hesitated. "The Pedregal family has been around for a long time. I imagine it would be interesting to sift through a few generations of papers."

"Is that what you were doing the other day, Doctor, when you were looking through the desk—searching through the family history?"

"No," he said seriously, and then his face broke into an attractive grin. "I told you. I was looking for a pocket calendar." Then he laughed aloud.

"Now it's my turn to ask what's wrong," she said.

"You don't like me very much, do you, Miss Ross?"

"And that amuses you?"

"It does only because I am really a very likable guy."

"I don't think about it one way or another," she answered coolly as she sipped her drink.

"I don't think that's correct."

"What do you mean?" She was becoming more agitated and began to feel sorry that she had come down to the patio early.

"You don't appear to be a person who thinks casually about anything. I think you feel definitely about all subjects and people—one way or another."

As if by cue or some silent prayer or command of her own, somewhere on the estate someone began strumming a guitar and singing. The voice raised in a crescendo of *canto hondo*—the beautiful lament of the gypsies, singing of extreme happiness webbed with soulful despair. Like the evening the song was beautiful and sad. Yet there was something promising in the sadness, some fulfillment so deep that the sadness the story told of was but a mere price to pay for having received it.

Ellen had turned her head in the direction of the music, and now as she faced the doctor again, she realized he had been watching her, his eyes gentle, his expression sensitive.

The scent of jasmine filled the air, and this, coupled by the gypsy chant in the background, suddenly intoxicated her.

He was taking a few steps toward her now, his eyes never leaving her face. She felt numbed—mesmerized by those eyes. If the others had not descended at that moment, he would have spoken to her. Instead he turned abruptly and retreated to the bar.

She was happy that they arrived at that point, chattering and innocent of the moment that had just passed. She was happy—and like the gypsy song—extremely sad all at the same time.

CHAPTER 9

It was very late when she decided to prepare for bed. She had no idea of how long she had been sitting in the chaise longue staring out into space. Dinner had been short but tedious. Joaquin was charming and talkative, but appeared rushed to leave the table and attend to additional preparations for the festival. Madama preened in the splendor of her scarlet silk dress, lifting her fingers every so often to admire her amethyst rings and then probing her neck to feel the grandeur of her amethyst necklace. She said very little, but what she did utter were cooing words of how elegant the festival would be.

Ellen felt very restless throughout the meal. She tried to keep a semblance of interest toward Joaquin's conversation, and yet her mind was very much on Dr. Bradshaw. She noticed that he ate very little, spoke nothing at all, and continued to throw her quick glances while poking at his own food. She realized he was paying no attention to Joaquin's chatter and wondered if Joaquin noted this.

While she was sitting in the chaise longue, her mind had wandered, from her appraisal work to the coming festival and then to Joaquin and the doctor. Disjointed thoughts—with no outcome.

She knew she should get some sleep because

she had planned to spend all of the following day in the library—hoping to finish the search for the documents. She was anxious to work directly on the paintings and terminate the assignment. But did she really want to leave the estate? She couldn't answer herself.

She finally settled herself in bed. Although she had left the windows ajar, she felt no breeze come through the open panes and she tossed frantically, trying to find that one unused spot in the bed-clothes that might have retained some coolness. At times her body quieted and she felt her inner self falling, down, deep into nowhere. Yet her outer senses would not let go, and she jumped, awakened to the heavy air, only to turn and start the process all over again.

Finally she sat up in bed. There was no need to try any further. She knew what was preying on her mind. There would be no peace for her that evening unless she went to the source of her problem. She had to see the blue room again, tarry in it, search it.

Without even bothering to look for her robe, she made her way to the door, opened it, and peered out. No one was about, and she acted quickly by walking farther down the landing to the large painting. Her back was to her own room as she tried to turn the large canvas to the left. For some reason it would not move. She tried again, frantically, wondering at the same time if she had been in her right senses that other night when she assumed she had entered a passage behind the wall which gave access to a beautiful room decorated in various hues of blue.

The sparks that suddenly flew through her eyes were red and yellow as she felt the sharp pain at the back of her head. There was no time to scream as the ornately tiled floor came up too quickly to her sinking body.

The light was fuzzy, but she knew that someone's profile stood before her.

"Drink this, it'll make you feel a bit stronger." Dr. Bradshaw's face was pleasant, and so was his smile. Sideward and almost wicked, she remembered, but pleasant.

"Dr. Bradshaw?" Her mind flashed back to the landing near her room. Someone had hit her at the back of the head.

"Come on. I thought for a moment you were happy to see me. I guess I was mistaken."

"I guess you were at that." She tried to raise herself from the divan, but her head throbbed heavily, and she had to lean back once more on the soft cushions.

"Drink this, I said. It'll strengthen you."

His eyes were tender and his voice soothing. But someone had hit her over the head, she could not help thinking repetitiously.

"Doctor, I want to go back to my room. And if you don't help me back I will attempt to go myself even if it means falling a dozen times on the way. Also, you can take that glass away from me. I don't intend to drink any of your medicinal brews. If you force me, I'll scream." Although who would hear me, she said to herself.

He rose from the seat beside her and crossed over to the table to reach for his pipe. His shoulders were massive, and she could not help but feel that same strange excitement that kept creeping into her being many times since her arrival when she thought of him. After he swung around to a single easy chair, he settled himself and then proceeded to light his pipe and eye her disapprovingly at the same time.

"Did you hear me, Dr. Bradshaw? I want to go back to my room."

"How could anyone help but hear you if you protest with such vehemence. Besides, why don't you call me Eric? It would be more cozy, wouldn't it?"

"I have no intention of calling you by your given name, nor becoming cozy. Now, will you help me back to my room, or must I try on my own?"

"You really should have that drink. The bullfighters consume that particular brew before entering the ring. It is supposed to fortify their courage, although I doubt you're lacking in that respect."

"I absolutely refuse to drink anything that you might offer me."

"I see," he said, again displaying the wicked grin. "You think I've put something in the glass."

"I didn't exactly say that," she retorted.

"You are quite illogical in your thinking, you know. Why would I rescue you from . . . whatever scrape you fell into, only to place you on my divan to poison you?"

"Who said anything about poisoning?" Her voice was slightly on the hysterical.

"Or drug you, or whatever you are thinking." He placed his pipe on the table tray and walked slowly over to her. From her reclined position he appeared gigantic and overpowering. Again he eyed her disapprovingly.

"What is the matter, Dr. Bradshaw? Am I interfering with your plans by not drinking that medicine?"

"It's not medicine. More of a tonic. But I can't deny that you are interfering. The question is now, what to do with you."

"I told you . . ."

"I know, I know. I'm quite hurt that you are not pleased at my hospitality," he said as he sat next to her once again.

She looked around her quickly. This must be a room in his own chalet, she thought. Then as her eyes rested on his face, again she said, "What are you going to do?"

"I'm just going to change the wet cloth on your head." He took the cloth from her and proceeded to wet it in a bowl near the divan. Then fully satisfied with its saturation, he wrung it and placed it over her forehead, this time covering her eyes as well.

As she moved it impatiently from her point of vision, she knew that he was smiling at her. He could not have struck her over the head. No, please let him not be the one, she asked silently.

"You did that on purpose," she said, referring to the cloth. There was less annoyance in her

voice now. She felt her face flushing uncontrolla-
bly.

"I certainly did," he answered. "And if I had
my way, you would stay blindfolded in my chalet
for the rest of your stay here."

"Then you are involved with something more
than you're telling?"

"Yes, I am. But it's not as sinister as you are
imagining, although it's very important—to many
people." His fingers were holding her chin now,
tugging gently, his voice crooning. "I did try to
dissuade you from staying. But you're a persistent
little wench. Persistent and curious. You are complicating matters, and I'm not sure what to do
about it."

She stared at him incredulously. He was admitting to being there for other reasons than everyone assumed. He was admitting to her—right to
her face—that she was in his way. He said it
wasn't anything sinister, yet what could it be?

Although she had been berating him since her
head had cleared, she felt very comfortable and
serene lying on the divan. Suddenly she wanted
to tell him about the room she had discovered.
But she couldn't, could she? He was involved
with something other than medical research. He
certainly didn't want her there. Something she
was doing was pulling against his plans. The
paintings? He did not want her to appraise the
paintings. The artwork would bring revenue to expand the ranch. Could he have been sent by another rancher to stall the development of the
land? A competitor. He could have been sent by a

competitor. And yet even thinking this way, he warmed her. His presence relaxed her and made her feel protected.

"Rest a moment," he was saying. "I'll get you something to eat. You hardly touched your dinner tonight, or hadn't you thought I noticed?"

"I . . . was listening to Joaquin's plans for the festival. I was also very restless."

"Persistent, curious, and unmanageable," she heard him say as he disappeared, most probably into the kitchen area.

She should make an attempt to leave. The pain in her head was not so pronounced now although she still felt dazed and shaky. She probably wouldn't make the climb to the villa, but she should at least try. She had to try. He had admitted being there under false pretenses. She couldn't condone that. And if she remained without trying to make a break, she would be condoning it.

She wanted so to stay, to have him soothe her, she thought as she slowly walked toward the front door. Why did he admit that she was interfering in his plans. If only he hadn't admitted it. . . . The room swayed. He's up to something. He admitted he was.

"Ellen." She heard him call her name just before she fell to the floor. "You vixen." He was whispering in her ear as he lifted her and carried her back to the divan. He placed her down gently, resting her head on the heap of soft pillows he had previously constructed for her. His head was close to hers. "What am I to do with you," he said as he stroked her hair.

Her lips were trembling. From the fall? He was so close. She wanted him, she knew she did. "Why did you admit it? Why?". .

"Admit?" he asked. "That I wanted you to remain blindfolded against any complications that may arise here?"

"You said that you are involved in something other than what we all know about."

"But nothing particularly sinister. Do you remember me saying that?"

"Meaning what, Dr. Bradshaw?"

"Eric!" He allowed his fingers to move away from her hair to stroke her face.

"Tell me, please. I must know if . . ." she couldn't continue.

"You must know if I'm a bad man or not, Ellen? Why—why does it matter?"

He was stroking her shoulder, his body leaning over her as she lay on the divan. She looked up at him, and their eyes met and held. Suddenly his fingers tightened around her arm, and then he was lifting her shoulders off the cushions as he brought her close to him. She could do nothing but call his name.

"Eric . . . Eric . . . I want . . ."

"What do you want, Ellen, tell me what you want." His face was buried in her hair, whispering to her, caressing her.

"Eric . . . I . . ."

"No, Ellen, no more fighting me, or fighting

each other. Come to me, Ellen, trust me; I adore you."

She surrendered to him then, to his mouth, to his hands, to his passion, and allowed the fire buried so long within her to surface freely.

She clung to him for a long time, wallowing in a realm of pure ecstasy that brings with it no definite thoughts except pure contentment.

He stroked her hair again as he smiled at her. "There is hope then, of your seeing me as a kind and benevolent gentleman rather than someone sinister?" he laughed.

She smiled back at him, happy that the game-playing was over.

"I'll tell you what," he continued. "If you promise to stay put, I'll get that nourishment I promised you. Then, young lady, I think it's time I had an honest talk with you. Persistent, curious, unmanageable, and stubborn. But you leave me no choice. Will you stay put?"

"I promise, Eric." Then, "Only if you level with me."

"Did I say stubborn?"

"Yes, you said stubborn."

"Just wanted to make sure," he said, retracing his steps to the kitchen.

She did stay put and felt snug ensconced on the softly tufted divan, with a silken robe—Eric's robe—discreetly covering her light gown.

As she looked around her she realized that the chalet must have been newly constructed because its furnishings were of modern design, yet everything was arranged to give the illusion of a lodge.

The carpeting had a high, plush, shaggy pile and was colored in waves of green and soft yellow so that it looked very much like a field of grass and clover. The divan was of deep gold velvet which matched exactly the hue of the heavy raw-silk draperies. The other chairs were also covered with velvet, but they ranged from muted green to mustard brown. Heavy dark-wood paneling made up the walls which focused on a large stone hearth at one end. All the individual lamps emerged from either stone or tree-branch bases. It was all so comforting, heavy, and protecting, yet elegant and pleasing.

He would dispel her fears now, this man who had already managed to fill her emotions to the brim of endurance. He could quell her trepidations and now make everything right. He emerged from an anteroom carrying a tray containing a variety of dishes.

"I must warn you for appearance' sake. Milta is away tonight on a visit to her family. But I doubt that anyone saw me rescuing the fair maiden from her enemy. And surely the enemy was too busy absconding from the scene of her shocking assault to notice my rescue."

"Why did you say 'her' assault, Eric?"

"Did I? Just a figure of speech. What were you doing out in that flimsy attire anyway?" He helped her sit up and placed the tray in front of her. Then he made himself comfortable on the carpeted floor beside her.

"I was looking for a stairway to the sky," she said flatly.

"Of course. I expect all good art appraisers to chase fantasies during the night. I take it you did not succeed in finding this staircase?"

"No. I'm afraid I was found first."

The wine he had brought her was the good-tasting white manzanilla of the region. It warmed her, though she needed no other warmth than having him sit near her as he was doing at that moment.

She smiled at him. Of course he couldn't have been the one who assaulted her. Now they would exchange honesties, she thought, and all the enigmas would be over soon.

"You are very fond of Amparo, Eric. You said you two go back a long way. Yet you've only been here a month?"

He looked up at her, his expression quite serious. "I was the doctor on duty at Amparo's birth," he said.

"But . . . does Joaquin know this? He never mentioned . . ."

"Amparo's mother was visiting her sister in London—she was English, you know. Joaquin was somewhere chasing rainbows at that time. Actually, my colleague signed the birth certificate, although I was the guy that actually delivered her. Joaquin has no knowledge of the situation, and . . . I didn't think it was necessary to mention it . . . for the time being."

"Why are you here, Eric?"

He looked up at her and smiled. "Ellen, would you believe me if I told you that it would be to your advantage to remain innocent of the situation?"

"But . . . you said you would level with me."

"I will, to a point. I am here looking into various clinics that are concerned with children's blood diseases. I thought I would combine that with . . . with another chore I had to deal with here in Seville. Something, Ellen, that is not devious, but that I feel safer keeping from you."

She looked at him blandly. Then her temper rose. "You are quite blunt, aren't you, Doctor?" she said quietly.

"What do you mean?"

"You're telling me flatly that you don't trust me."

"No—you are unmanageable, I was right. I didn't mean it that way."

The knock that came then at the door startled both of them.

"Stay put." He recovered before she did and walked quickly to the door.

"But . . ."

"Don't fret. You were hurt and I helped you. There is nothing wrong with your presence here."

"Eric, sorry for the intrusion. Mother is not feeling well, nothing serious, but I would feel better if you stopped in to see her." Joaquin's voice was thick with heavy sleep as he stepped through the door. But his eyes narrowed and his face hardened as he saw Ellen, who was still sitting on the divan.

"Well, I have intruded, haven't I?" he said coldly.

"Miss Ross has met with an accident. Since it wasn't serious, I felt that I could revive her here without alarming the household."

"What happened to you?" he asked her, meeting her gaze with hostile eyes.

"She merely fell during a nocturnal stroll in the garden when she wouldn't sleep," the doctor answered.

"Do you usually walk about barefoot and robeless?" asked Joaquin.

He was too sharp to digest the story, thought Ellen. Why couldn't Eric tell him the truth? He should be informed that someone was prowling in the night and assaulting people on his own estate.

"I just went to the kitchen for some milk, not intending to go out. Suddenly I felt that I wanted a breath of air." She was annoyed at herself for taking up Eric Bradshaw's story.

"Perhaps you will help me return her to the villa," Eric was asking Joaquin.

"Let me take the tray from you." The doctor was bending over her now, lifting the dishes from her lap. His lips moved as he faced her. She thought he was trying to say "Trust me" but she wasn't sure.

She suddenly became quite vexed with the situation. Eric Bradshaw hadn't told her anything about himself—except that he had delivered Amparo. He knew Joaquin's diseased wife. How well? she wondered. Now he didn't trust her enough to tell her what he was really doing in Spain.

There was nothing more that she could do but have the two men lead her slowly to the villa.

Hardly anyone spoke on the short walk, and her head reeled with dizziness as she realized that she could not have made it on her own had she been able to leave the chalet earlier.

"I would not do anything strenuous for two days," Eric was saying as he was about to take leave of her at her room. Joaquin had followed them and since he stood next to the doctor, she could only murmur a brief "Thank you" as she closed the door behind her.

CHAPTER 10

She had decided to relax awhile on the chaise longue, trying to find the physical and mental balance that only rest could bring. Her head throbbed again, probably as a result of the walk back to the villa, she thought.

Eric had seemed quite anxious about her on the way back; he had held onto her arm tightly, his face grave with concern. And this concern, she knew, was more for the state of her mental being than her physical discomfort. He realized that she still doubted him. How did it disturb him? she wondered. As someone who had feelings for her, or as one who in guilt was disturbed at having his cover penetrated?

What ground she had covered in the last two hours. She had gone from restlessness to physical pain, through anger and emotional ecstasy, to disappointment and restlessness again. A full circle which inevitably left her where she had begun. She was certain of one thing. She would not rely on Eric. Aside from the deep attraction she held for him, she had been too ready to step back and have him take the burden of everything from her mind. She had sat back on the divan and prepared to tell him about the tower room and all her other doubts concerning the family. For a fleeting moment she had wanted him to take on the role Sandy had always played in her life, and that would not do for her now. It would only make her reap the benefits from his endeavors as a parasite nourishes from its anchor. She would also stay untouched from any harm and mourn detached if he were to err or fall into negative circumstances.

There had been no spark with Sandy. What intensity could be passed between them if she did not share life with him—life is all the torment, glory, and responsibility that involvement offers. She would not sit back and allow Dr. Bradshaw to live for her. If their relationship was meant to continue, they would meet somewhere along the way. Now there were a few important matters that needed tending to, and she would do it alone, without leaning on anyone.

Her head was just beginning to clear when she heard the tap on the door. Her hands gripped the sides of the chaise. There was not to be any peace for her that night. Was the person who struck her now determined to follow her to her bedroom to cast the final blow? She knew that she was overdramatizing, yet although her head had cleared, her nerves were still touchy.

Ellen rose from the chaise and leaned heavily near the crack of the door.

"Who is it? What do you want?" Her voice showed all of her emotions as it cracked and strained.

"Ellen, it's Eric. I want to talk to you. Let me in, please."

"I'm sorry, Doctor. Unless you have some means

of breaking down this door, it will remain closed, especially to you."

"Please, Ellen. I must see you."

She remembered him saying that it would be safer if he did not tell her what he was doing at the villa. He had no trust for her either.

"I am in need of no medical attention. The best thing you could do for me is to leave me alone." Her voice broke again, and she tried in vain to hold back the tears that were welling up in her eyes. She had seen Joaquin's faults and weaknesses, and her feelings for him had diminished. Now she realized that Eric Bradshaw could be mixed up in some serious wrongdoings, and yet her feelings for him would not die. He was being unkind to her by suggesting that he did not trust her. Yet she wanted him. She still wanted him.

"Will you leave me alone, please."

"You are obstinate, you know. Headstrong, self-willed, and stubborn."

Her ear was tight against the door slit, and she could hear him heave a heavy sigh of exasperation.

"Will it help matters if I tell you that I am also looking for documents here at the villa—papers that will reaffirm a legacy that will help many sick children?"

Her mind clicked—shaping tableaux, quickly summarizing past events—and although her thoughts did not form any conclusions, it seemed right to unlatch the door after what he had just said. He was looking for documents that would help children. Part of a legacy. That meant—it meant something. Her mind was thick with facts and weariness. She opened the door. As he walked swiftly past her into the room, his face was hardened and he glowered at her, almost with hatred.

"I don't know what this all means," she stammered, "but what you just said is significant of something, though my mind is so muddled I don't know what it is yet."

"If you weren't so completely mistrusting, I would have been willing to explain the significance to you without having to announce it outside your door at the waiting ears of anyone."

He was truly exasperated with her, yet all the characteristics he just bestowed upon her with his verbal lashings were not her own. Or were they? Was she not the trusting soul who had allowed Sandy to lead her through life while she followed unquestioningly? Had she really changed that much in the last few weeks? She had never mistrusted anyone before, nor had she ever shown any strong will of her own toward anything. She tightened her lips to obliterate the smile forming across her mouth. Eric Bradshaw would never understand this one private moment taken from the complicated situation they were both experiencing. Yet her stay at the villa was not a separate part of her life. She had stood at the crossroads of change in her own feelings even before she parted with Sandy. Now it seemed that she was finally released from the chains that held her as a dependent, clinging being. She doubted that she was really obstinate or stubborn. But she had become her own person, questioning when her mind deemed it necessary, more self-reliant than she had ever been before.

"You would make a wench of a wife," the doctor snapped, still expounding furiously. Then, as if realizing what he had said, he flushed slightly, his manner quieting. He looked miserable and upset.

"Please sit down." She motioned to the sitting area and then put on a blue silk robe. Sitting across from him, she noticed that he did not look directly at her as he spoke. He was cooling toward her again, she thought.

"I'd better start at the beginning," he said. "You already know that I delivered Amparo at a hospital in London. I was in residency at the time. Lucinda, Joaquin's wife, was thrilled that the baby was born healthy. She had lost her first child to a rare blood disease, so she was extremely delighted at Amparo's birth. She kept writing me after she returned to Spain—keeping me informed of Amparo's growth and health. The child was doing beautifully. After two years passed, I received a very serious letter from Lucinda. I think she was worried about her own health. She claimed that she owned a large piece of land adjacent to the Pedregal estate. She stated that she had written a will requesting that the land be used to build a children's clinic that could concentrate on the particular blood disease that took her first child."

"And you're here looking for the legal documents that Lucinda wrote?" Ellen asked quietly.

"That's correct," he answered, looking directly at her now.

"But even if you did find the document, who would provide the funds to build the clinic?"

"That's the second problem at hand that I'm not clear about. She also stated in her letter that I shouldn't worry about the end of it as she was sure the beautiful bouquet of flowers would provide the funds for the building and equipment. I didn't understand that statement. She seemed to be rambling. She was probably very ill when she wrote the letter. Of course I would have to do some extra fund raising to provide additional money to staff the clinic and continue its maintenance."

"In other words, you would direct the proceedings?" the girl asked.

"That's what she wanted. I've been traveling all over the south soliciting promises for these funds from prominent families. Of course I've been telling these people that I'm looking for a site for the clinic. I can't mention where it would be unless I find the document."

"Why don't you just ask Joaquin for it?"

"Come El— . . ." he let the last syllable of her name die with his lowered voice. This hesitancy stung at her heart. She was wary of the story he was telling, but she did love him, she was certain of that. No matter, this situation would be seen to its end, and then she would leave that place. She had found a balance and inner awareness of herself there. For that she was most grateful. But she had allowed her already scarred emotions to take on a new breath of love and yet she felt that any renewed pain stemming from disappointment or unfulfillment was too much to ask of herself at that time.

"I've given Joaquin enough chances to admit to the document," he was continuing. "I've even approached his desire to spread the family name, thinking that offering the land to a benevolent cause would appeal to his—arrogance."

"That's unkind," she uttered, although she understood fully what he meant.

"I'm not sure what I'll do now. The clinic would help many children."

"Why . . . why did you say that I was interfering with your plans?" she asked.

"Well . . ." she thought he was about to smile, but he caught himself and his face remained serious. "I just felt that once you gave approval on the Perez paintings, the land would be developed to expand the ranch. Finding the document then would be too late. I don't think I could sue on behalf of the deceased Lucinda."

"I don't understand one thing," she said. "Why do you need the document? Can't you merely show Joaquin Lucinda's letter?"

Here he rose and stood with his back to her, as he gazed silently out the window into the blackness of the night.

"Why are you hesitating in answering that question?" she asked, hating the urgency in her own voice.

With that he swung around, his eyes becoming narrow slits as he asked, "Do you ever trust anyone? I mean, have you ever in your life trusted one human being?"

His sudden gush of anger subsided quickly as he saw how his words had stung at her.

She lifted her head as high as she could to try to feign composure and said, "Is there anything else you want to tell me?"

She thought he was about to reach for her at that moment as they stared at one another. She suddenly felt that she wanted to run to him also. Yet they both remained where they were.

"I . . . the letter from Lucinda was burned in a fire that broke out at the hospital," he said sheepishly as he walked to the door. Then, "Is there anything that you need? You'll be all right, you know."

"What do you mean?"

"Your eyes are not dilated, and your breathing seems normal. You are favoring your left shoulder, but hot compresses will see to that, since you're not favoring it too much. Unless you have another bruise somewhere that is not noticeable to my eyes, I think a good night's rest would do the trick. Would you like me to give you something to make you sleep?"

"No, I don't think that I'll need anything."

"I see. Still think I'm dishonest," he said more as a declaration than a question.

She didn't have time to answer him as he swiftly opened and closed the door behind him and left her room.

* * *

She felt exhausted, but her head had stopped
its throbbing. She wondered if it was sheer hys-
teria on her part to attempt the plan that she had
in mind. She checked her watch on the bedside
table and saw that it was 5:00 A.M. The few hours
of sleep she had had were not long enough to
have completely healed her tired body, but were
adequate enough to make her feel a bit better
than the night before. She would have to do this
now while everyone slept. Some of the workmen
on the ranch were sure to be up, but the household would be quiet for at least another two
hours.

This time she dressed completely so that if anyone caught her on the landing to or from her des-
tination, she could always say that she was hungry
and seeking an early breakfast.

She reached into her lower drawer and produced the little black bag that contained her
working tools. Now she was ready—except for one
decision. She had two destinations in mind: The
tower room and the library. Thinking about the
cleanliness of the room atop the silo, she realized
that Louisa must make daily excursions there to
keep the room in proper order. It would be best
for her to get her business over with in that area,
as her presence in the library would not be too
suspicious since she had been working there all
week.

She made her way out to the landing and stood
before the large painting. It had to work on the
first try, she thought, or her timing would be off
schedule. She couldn't help but look over her

shoulder as she wanted no recurrence of the night before. She never did tell the doctor what she was doing when she had been struck over the head. He had covered so beautifully with Joaquin, and so obviously that she imagined he knew she had been up to no good somewhere on the estate. She never questioned how he managed to find her and take her to his chalet. Unless . . . no, she wouldn't think that he could have struck her. He wouldn't have admitted all he did if he had struck her to prevent her from visiting the room. As far as she was concerned, he did not even know the room existed.

She moved the painting to the left, and the wall panel slid open. Then she passed through the opening and pressed the knob for the panel to close behind her. It was easy so far, she thought. As she began climbing the spiral staircase, her mind kept hovering over Eric Bradshaw and the way he acted when she had mentioned Lucinda's letter. Of course he could be telling the truth about the fire, she thought. But it was too convenient, all too convenient an excuse. Yet he *had* been prodding Joaquin to do something benevolent with the land. She remembered their conversation during her first night at dinner with the family. It might be true then. She felt a pang of guilt as she thought of how harsh she had been with the doctor. But if what he said was true, it certainly placed Joaquin in a bad light. Could his arrogance and need for grandeur be so strong that he would have disregarded Lucinda's wish for a clinic?

As she neared the top of the staircase, she thought of Joaquin's relationship with Amparo. She had never seen him with the child, nor had the child ever been included at a family dinner gathering. Joaquin ignored Amparo, she guessed—ignored and resented her.

She had reached the top of the landing and faced the door of the tower room. It had never occurred to her that the door might be locked, but as she tried it, the door swung open easily into the tower suite.

She stood at the threshold a moment and hesitated. A mild aroma of cigarette smoke filled her nostrils. Her eye caught an ashtray atop the end table by the easy chair. As she walked over to it, she noticed that three rolled cigarettes, half smoked, had been extinguished in it. The windows of the tower were not open, and the room had evidently retained the smoke fumes. She wouldn't open the windows, she thought, or touch anything more than her work necessitated.

The painting was the same one that had caught her eye the first time she visited the room. It was easily released from its hanging on the wall, and as she looked closely at it now, she guessed that it was exactly what she thought it would be. But being dedicated to her special field, she knew that further tests would be necessary before she could be sure.

The frame needed a little extra prodding to detach it from the canvas, but she accomplished the chore without too much trouble by using one of the levers in her kit. Now her eye immediately sought the extreme left of the canvas and there, as she had anticipated, were the tiny drops of white paint, like little balls that might have fallen by accident from the artist's brush. Either that or since the study was centered around a bouquet of flowers, these could be seen by the layman as small fluffs of petals that broke away from the original cluster. But Ellen knew better what the droplets signified.

Now she turned the painting over and examined the unused area of the canvas. She produced a magnifying glass from her bag, and it showed her that the coarse fibers of the canvas material were formed by three varied colors of tan, one almost bordering on orange.

She looked at the painting face-on again. This time from her kit she produced a glove that was made of very fine gauze. With her finger she traced the outline of the flowers that abundantly made up the spray contained in the sea-blue vase. As she had guessed, each flower was raised at least a quarter of an inch, as if they had been sculpted instead of painted onto the canvas, and this was not far from the truth.

The two pigment tests that followed were just to reaffirm what she already knew. Lucinda's beautiful tower retreat contained a late Vargas painting. And because it was one of the artist's latest endeavors, it was indeed valuable. She could see why a woman who occupied that lovely room would cherish any of Vargas's work, because he had painted the beauty of life—garden scenes and rambling meadows and flowers—always flowers. Therefore the tragedy of how his own life ended was even more shocking to his followers and the world in general. Vargas was totally blind for two years before his death, and in those two years he had produced four paintings which he had signed in braille. Lucinda Pedregal had owned one of these four studies. The amazing factor in Vargas's later works which showed prominently in Lucinda's painting was that due to his blindness the artist eventually found it necessary to use his fingers to mold many of his subjects, therefore using great amounts of paint on the canvas. The protruding flowers Ellen had touched were a result of this. The droplets of paint on the left side of the canvas were Vargas's signature. She had seen them enough in books during her studies, and being so touched by the story of the young artist, she had practically memorized the pattern and distance between each symbol.

Her actions had to be fast now. After the pigment tests proved positive, she quickly placed the canvas back into its frame and hung the picture back on the wall.

She cast a quick look again at the ashtray containing the extinguished cigarettes and then made her way quickly down the staircase.

There was one more chore to complete on the Perez paintings, and then she would have the finishing chapters to the story.

CHAPTER 11

The day had begun too soon for her. She wished that there could be some suspension of time for the rest of the world so she could catch up to herself physically and mentally.

The sun that poured through the windows of the *antesala* was bright and pleasingly warm. The excessive summer heat seemed to have passed, and autumn had suddenly been born—a pity that no one there had had time to feast in its welcome. But the festival would take care of that today. The estate would come alive that afternoon and swarming over its grounds would be gay and happy people. She wondered then if the walls of the great house could withstand the echo of laughter ringing through its boundaries.

Ellen ate ravenously, but reprimanded herself silently for not having confessed to Joaquin or Madama that she was indeed accosted in their household. She wondered why Eric Bradshaw did not insist that she get to the bottom of whom her attacker had been. As she thought of him now, she wondered how her own lack of faith in him had affected his feelings toward her. Certainly any feelings he had shown her the other evening in his chalet were shattered by now.

"It's your own fault, Dr. Bradshaw," she said aloud to the empty dining room.

If he had leveled with her in the beginning, she thought, they could have worked together. Yet she had been a stranger to him, and he had had his own pressures of masquerading as something he was not in order to preserve the dying wish of the tragic Lucinda.

Looking back now, she could see that he had always held some concern for her. At their first meetings, he had been gruff and tried to disillusion her. But later in his chalet he had admitted that he did not want her involved in the complicated activities that were unfolding at the villa. Then when someone had struck her, he had carried her back to his chalet and administered to her. No, she had not been very understanding to Eric Bradshaw, and she did not blame him if he cooled again toward her.

It was late morning now and time that she returned to her room and dressed. Her festival outfit had been placed, pressed and elegant, in her closet. As she took it out and laid it carefully on her bed, she suddenly felt saddened and very much alone. A festival in Spain should be gay and filled with happiness.

From the feeling in her heart she wondered how that day could bring her happiness. And coupled with the loneliness was an awareness of fear. With all the other things on her mind, she had not allowed it to take a prominent part of her thoughts, yet someone had struck her the other night. Someone realized that she had knowledge of the tower room. And with this realization came the knowledge that Ellen Ross was on to something that the person did not want known. She had a strong feeling that she would learn the identity of that person by the end of the festival.

She raised her skirts and slowly made her way down the staircase, through the patio, and out to the area behind the tower where they were all to assemble. The house was empty as she passed through it. Everyone else, even Amparo—who was not to be contained—had left the house before her.

As she now raced out to the lawn, she could not help but feel some of the excitement of the day. The seamstress had done magnificent work with her dress. The bodice hugged her figure, with the neckline dropping down to a conservative but flattering curve and then tapering to narrow straps that showed her still-tanned shoulders. The waist of the dress was tiny, but just below that the material flared out to a wide skirt layered with flounces of white-lace ruffle before stopping at her ankles. Most of the staff would also wear the traditional skirts of Seville which stopped at the ankle line. Only Madama would wear the long train of Granada since her family line dated back to that region of Spain.

At first she had felt a little foolish donning the beautifully made lace mantilla that was to hang delicately from the tortoise-shell comb in her hair. Yet as she placed the red rose Amparo had given her firmly in front of the comb, she began to feel a little of the aura of the day. She had to admit that she did look elegant.

She was one of the last to arrive at the assembly

area. The acre of land just behind the tower which led to the corrals had been transformed into a carnival setting with red and white tents spotting the grounds.

The grooms had gathered a number of mounts from the stables, and the horses now pranced and scuffed the earth with their hoofs as if anxious to get on with their role in the festivities. Ellen immediately spied Amparo who was sitting in the carriage beside Madama, trying very hard, however unsuccessfully, to emulate the old woman's proud and stately attitude. The child's expression broke, however, as soon as she spied Ellen, and with a squeal of delight she scrambled from the carriage, her own lace mantilla flying behind her as she ran to meet her companion. Ellen and the child embraced and exchanged compliments on each other's dresses. Amparo had emerged in a pink dress with white dots and pink and white flounces making up the tiers of her skirt.

"Miss Ross," the fleeting moment of gaiety was suddenly shattered by Madama's icy voice. "We are already quite late in beginning the procession. If you would interest Amparo in getting back into the carriage and find your own mount, we can proceed. With whom are you coupled to ride?"

"I . . . don't know," Ellen faltered.

"Well, if you were here early with the rest of us you wouldn't be delaying us now," Madama continued haughtily.

"Madama, Miss Ross is scheduled to share my mount." The voice was that of Eric Bradshaw, who seemed to have appeared from nowhere sitting high on a proud roan.

He reined his mount to stop in front of her, and before she knew what was happening, Felix had placed a mounty trip at her feet and was helping Ellen to sit sidesaddle behind the doctor. As she turned her head, she saw Louisa and the rest of the staff coupling themselves in a similar fashion.

"For a moment I thought I was expected to ride my own mount in the procession," she said as if to herself.

"Why the concern . . . don't you ride?" Eric asked.

"Yes, I do. I was just thinking that no one ever bothered to inquire whether I did or not."

"That's because you weren't going to ride alone. So the fact that you are about to accuse someone of not being considerate is unfounded," he said. Then he threw her a quick glance over his shoulder and gave her one of his wide grins.

They had started so soon, she thought. The day had just begun and they were already at odds with each other.

"Hold on tightly to my waist now, and we'll get into position," he continued as he put the horse into a canter and made a stance behind the carriage as they waited for the rest of the mounts to get into position.

"Madama looks quite regal today," she commented, trying to hold onto some semblance of even chatter.

"Yes. As usual, she's bedecked in all of her fine jewels and sitting regally in her chariot while

Joaquin, poor devil, becomes a scavenger in his endeavors to keep up the image of the family name."

"Are they really that badly off?"

"So it seems. Like many of the prominent families of the area, the Pedregals have a beautiful home, a good amount of land and cattle, but lack ready currency. They probably could get along except for Madama's desire to increase the size of the estate."

"Of course it's Joaquin's desire also," she added, remembering Felix's affirmation of this that morning near the bullring.

"I'm not always sure of that," he answered. "Oh, yes, he's pompous—always will be. Yet every so often, I see him quieting, engrossed by something very deep—some memory perhaps that touches him and that's stronger than all of this." The conversation stopped for a few minutes as they each reflected on his words. Then turning to give her another quick glance over his shoulder, he said, "By the way, you probably wondered how you came to be in my chalet the other night. I had come over to the villa to talk to you. When I arrived on the landing I saw you sprawled on the floor. I could have taken you directly to your room, but as I smelled some foul play, I decided my chalet would be better. It was a risk. I never thought I'd make it without running into someone. But . . . it was late . . . and we did make it after all."

"Thank you for your gallantry, doctor," she answered coolly.

He threw her another swift glance and asked, "What were you doing on that part of the landing at that time of night anyway?"

"I was looking for a secret passage," she answered quietly.

His roar of laughter was so spontaneous and loud that a number of heads turned in their direction.

"Well, that reaffirms my decision," he guffawed.

"And what is that, may I ask, doctor?"

"When I left your room last evening, I didn't go directly to sleep," he said. "I was disturbed and felt that something very important had to be decided. It didn't take me very long to make the decision. You see, you will have to become my wife. There is no doubt in my mind about that now."

His statement had left her gasping, but she managed to say, "You are quite sure of yourself, aren't you?"

"It's all very simple. I couldn't possibly go through life worrying where you were or what escapade you were getting into. My work is too serious. I would not be able to feel at ease unless you were at my side. Besides, with your willful character you will need me as a stability factor."

At that moment—and thankfully, she thought, as she was too numb to answer her companion—Felix took his place at the head of the procession and blew the long medieval horn that was to start the festivities. The old man put his mount to a trot down the narrow road between the tents. He was followed by Madama and Amparo in their carriage. Then came Eric with Ellen sharing the roan, the girl's skirt spread elegantly over the horse's hind. Following them were the other members of the staff, the women being coupled with some of the ranch supervisors. From somewhere Ellen heard a brass quartet playing the strains for a majestic *pase doble*, the music depicting the very courage and pride of the Spanish people. As they approached the bullring, Ellen noticed that scaffolding had been constructed around its perimeter to provide benches for the guests who had already taken their seats.

"I had no idea that all these people were invited," she exclaimed.

"My poor Ellen. Your hours have been spent poking through musty library shelves and roaming the halls at night looking for secret passages."

"Now you are laughing at me," she said. "I'm beginning to find this event exciting. If only . . . that one question would be solved, I would be more at ease."

"And that is . . . ?"

"Someone did strike me. Someone knew I was getting close."

"To what?"

She had gained a lot of knowledge that morning when she visited the tower suite and the library. Yet she wasn't quite ready to divulge anything she had learned. She would wait—at least until after the festival.

"I was evidently getting close to something that whoever struck me didn't want divulged."

"Well, nothing more will happen today. I doubt that the Pedregals will let anything stand in the way of their glory. Smile, my pretty, we are about to enter the ring," he said as he motioned the horse to speed up.

The music was slow and regal as Felix's mount entered the inner circle of the bullring. Here the old man acknowledged the guests by doffing his plumed hat and bowing his head to the stands. The visitors rose to their feet and applauded as the remainder of the family entourage followed and also circled the ring. Madama raised her hand to wave serenely to her guests, her gestures slow and self-assured. Amparo wavered between expressions of extreme glee and a look of guilt toward Madama, as if fearful of showing too much happiness.

Felix finally pulled his horse to a halt and quickly dismounted. With an agile stride of a far younger man, he approached the carriage, which had also stopped, and helped Madama and Amparo down and to their seats in the front tier of the stands. Ranch hands appeared from wooden barriers around the inside of the ring to help the others dismount and to lead away the horses.

Ellen realized that there seemed to be a large staff where the guests could observe them, while the house staff had remained small. It would be typical of Madama to be sure the guests viewed the Pedregals as an affluent family. She looked over at the woman now who was seated in the splendor of her green festival dress, nodding regally, her diamonds glistening in the afternoon sun.

She was not yet able to shake the uneasiness

she felt earlier that someone had wished her harm. It had probably been more of a warning to mind her own business that had prompted the attacker than anything more serious. She was sure that if they had wished her permanent harm, they would have found a way. Yet someone had struck her, and that someone was very likely sitting near her right now.

She tried to rid herself of all these troublesome thoughts so that she could better enjoy the festival. She wondered then if she kept repeating them in her mind so that she would not think of the statement that Eric Bradshaw had made to her. He had asked her to marry him. Of course he had said it in his own sarcastic manner—was he teasing her? She would not think about it. Had he really asked her to marry him?

The trumpets of the small, hired quartet began shrieking the beginning of another *pase doble*. The gates of the *corrida* suddenly opened, and three men emerged, one walking slightly ahead of the others. To Ellen's amazement the leader of the three was Joaquin, elegantly attired in a suit of lights, the traditional uniform of the Spanish matador. His short jacket was of white satin glistening with jeweled stones of gold and amber. The satin trousers were skintight, stopping just at the ankle to show pink stockings that fit snugly into the black ballet skimmers. A black *montera* covered his head, and slung over his shoulder was the heavily embroidered cape which encircled the curve of his right arm. The other two men were similarly dressed, but their jackets were less adorned.

The three of them fell into step with the heaviness of the music, their faces drawn and serious. Yet their gait was grand and majestic, similar to proud monarchs taking survey of their newly conquered lands. The feeling of arrogance was in the air, but for some reason this was not offensive. Instead, pride and courage permeated the atmosphere, and this was somehow exhilarating, even to Ellen.

The procession continued across the red sand and halted in front of Madama and the first tier of seats. With a quick gesture Joaquin swung the ornate cape from his shoulder, and one of the other men took it and placed it over the railing in front of Amparo and her grandmother. The older woman was to be queen of the day, and she appeared most prepared for her role.

The *pase doble* ceased and after a few minutes of silence a single trumpet sounded, heralding the entrance of a black Miura bull into the ring. Joaquin walked behind one of the small wooden barriers and watched his companions make a few passes with their pink and gold capes, swirling and turning as if trying to agitate the beast. Eric explained to Ellen that this was an important moment in the bullfight, as Joaquin would be watching how the bull charged and if the animal favored one of its horns rather than the other in lunging toward the men. Discerning the idiosyncrasies of the bull in these first few minutes of the bullfight could mean the difference between life and death for the matador.

The trumpets sounded again and the two *toreros* left the bullring and took their positions behind one of the wooden barriers. The bull stood alone, stamping and scuffing the red earth and now fully agitated. Suddenly Joaquin emerged from another wooden barrier, his two hands clutching the ends of his pink and gold cape. At first he stood quite still. Then arching his back he raised his voice in a series of taunts, almost mimicking the grunting sounds of the animal itself.

"*Ahhhha, toro,*" he yelled. "*Venga, toro, ahhha.*"

He then made a run toward the bull, who in turn caught the sudden movement and advanced for attack. When the two were almost within centimeters of each other, Joaquin spread out his cape and stepped to one side so that the bull lunged under the extended material, snorting and angry that he had missed his goal. Joaquin turned quickly, beginning a series of veronica passes, holding the cape extended in his two hands and to one side of his body, while the bull lunged forward, the cape swirling over its back.

The audience was silent, and Ellen could feel the subdued tension exuding from the stands. Joaquin looked most attractive in the ring, his tanned face serious, yet proud. There was no false arrogance in his being. He was performing excellently, using his skill and knowledge of the animal to entice and confuse him. Any of the accolades that the crowd extended to the matador with their applause was well deserved indeed.

Ellen glanced quickly over at Madama and noticed that an expression of extreme pleasure covered the woman's face over her son's agility in the ring. The girl could not help but feel a little sorry for the young landowner. From what Felix had said to her, Joaquin was forced to leave a career in bullfighting to fill in as head of the estate for his deceased father. He had inherited the task of placating Madama's demands to expand the estate and to prove to the people of Seville that the Pedregals were indeed the foremost family in the area.

She looked back at Joaquin again, and the seriousness and innocence in his face as he met the ultimate in danger somehow tore at her. He seemed to have great interest in the bulls. She wondered if Eric had been correct in saying that Joaquin may not be the greedy landowner seeking more status and more grandeur for his estate. Perhaps away from Madama's haughty influence, he could have been quite a formidable gentleman. And more than that, he could now be at peace with himself.

CHAPTER 12

The banderilla sticks had been placed, and the trumpets sounded for a third time. Joaquin handed his cape to one of the *toreros* and took in its stead the small red muleta that was heaped over the matador's sword. But, instead of advancing toward the animal, he walked slowly over to the stands. Although it first appeared that he would stop before his mother, he moved his position to stand instead in front of Ellen. He bowed deeply and removed his hat as he spoke.

"Señorita, will you honor me by standing, please."

Eric Bradshaw quickly took hold of Ellen's arm and urged her up.

Joaquin continued speaking. "I will conquer the fierceness of this animal with all the courage of my forefathers. I do this in your honor today and for all the gentleness and grace that you possess. I do this also in memory of someone who, like you, represented everything that was good. To her memory and to you I dedicate this bull."

With that, Joaquin turned and tossed his hat over his shoulder. It was directed so close to Ellen that she could not help but catch it. Again she heard applause, and Eric explained to her that the gesture of catching the hat would bring Joaquin luck.

The faenas with the muleta that Joaquin executed were even more thrilling than his work with the cape. At one point he had confused the bull to such an extent that he was able to kneel in front of the stunned animal and place his hand on the bull's forehead. Ellen caught her breath as the young man made the final plunge with the sword and finally conquered the bull.

The brass quartet could hardly be heard amid the cheers of the guests as they rose to their feet and hailed the man to glory. Joaquin had recovered his hat from Ellen and was now walking proudly around the ring, bowing and gathering flowers that were tossed to him from friends and acquaintances who had optimistically taken them along to the event.

Joaquin had had his moment of glory, and Ellen was pleased. Somehow it seemed to her that his glories had been few in recent years.

The girl was about to relax, happy that the dangerous *corrida* was over and that Joaquin had proved triumphant. Suddenly, however, her eyes caught Madama looking in her direction, hostility flashing across her face. After all, Joaquin had committed an unforgivable sin. He had dedicated the bull, and therefore his triumph, to a perfect stranger—and to the memory of . . . was he thinking of Lucinda? Madama was resentful. Had she also resented Joaquin's love for Lucinda?

The atmosphere exploded into an array of gaiety. The day was grand, and Joaquin had triumphed.

The tents had been set up with tables containing every variety of food. Plates were laden with the best Spanish hors d'oeuvres available. These were chicken croquettes browned and succulent, salads of potatoes chopped very fine and mixed with prisms of red and green peppers and whipped in a heavy white cream. Bulls' liver was cut into cubes and dipped in a thick gravy containing black piquant herbs. There were shrimp and small squid in green sauce and small *cigala* crabs to be plucked and devoured. The wine was white manzanilla and sherry from Jerez. Later, roasts, lobster, and ham would be served.

The chairs in the tents were all placed in a semicircle and after eating buffet style, the guests would join in the entertainment of song and dance. Gypsy groups from the Triana section of Seville were hired for each tent, and they started their low lamentations of *canto hondo* and gay fandango dancing as soon as people began entering the tents.

Everyone was arrayed in festival outfits, the women wearing yards of flounces and mantillas, while the men were bedecked in *trajes cortos* of brown or black trousers with short vest jackets and flat, wide-brimmed hats.

Eric Bradshaw accompanied Ellen and Amparo from one tent to the next, so they could taste the *tapas* and beverages at each of them.

"The guests look so festive. I'm really beginning to relax," Ellen commented as they strolled down the roadway between the tents.

"The Pedregals are known for their fine festivals. By the way, did I mention how lovely you look in your frock?"

"Thank you," she turned and smiled at him. "The seamstress did put a lot of work into these dresses."

"And, young lady, you haven't answered my question yet," he grinned back at her.

"Your question?"

"Will you be my wife, Ellen?"

"You don't really know anything about me, Eric."

"We'll have many years together to give me a chance to learn all about you."

"And when you learn that I'm not what you expect?"

"Oh, I'm sure there are many hidden facets to you." He turned now and took both her hands in his.

"Eric, do you realize that we have spent most of our relationship bickering and feuding?"

"We have only because you're so obstinate." He was laughing now. "And we'll probably have more feuds waiting for us in the future. But I can't think of anyone else I'd rather feud with . . . or love . . . or take care of. It won't be an easy future, Ellen. I'm quite dedicated to my work. Yet I don't see you thriving in a complacent way of life—living a scheduled existence and being led and helped over easy hurdles. I think something inside you would burst if you had to live in that way. You're too much of a fighter and too independent of mind."

She had lived that way though—and she did

burst out of it. But would she again slip back to the dependency? If she did, it would not be good for him, since he would need an independent woman to balance the dedication he needed for his work.

Again, she did not have to answer him. As usual in their few intimate conversations, they were interrupted. And, as a matter of course, she couldn't help but be relieved. She was sure of her love for this man, but so many things plagued her. She still felt the insecurity of her break with Sandy. She wasn't sure of her strength and how she would react if, once committed, something would go wrong with this new relationship. She was frightened to take the step. Yet she cared for him so much. Could she have finally found her Utopia? After the last few weeks she mistrusted the feeling of joy that she wanted so badly to permeate her being at that moment.

"Miss Ross—Ellen." It was Joaquin, who had walked up to them. "Please take Amparo over to Jime Ortega's tent. She must perform her dance immediately. The guitarist is waiting for her."

He left them no time to personally congratulate him on his finesse in the bullring as he turned and immediately walked over to one of the larger tents.

"He's preoccupied about something," Eric commented.

"He should be enjoying the day. He performed so beautifully in the ring. It's really unfortunate that he couldn't pursue a career in bullfighting."

"He had the burden of the estate, Ellen. That ... and ..."

"And ... something more?"

"I'm not sure. Let's get Amparo over to the Ortega tent. Jime is the reigning sovereign of bullfighters in Spain and an old school chum of Joaquin's. He's always been allowed to have his own tent at the Pedregal gala. He hires the best gypsy group of dancers in the area and also serves the best table. Of course Madama is thrilled that she can claim so famous a personage to be part of her festival."

The young matador's tent was the most festive that they had visited. Colorful lanterns were strung in abundance across the ceiling from corner to corner.

When they entered, one of the gypsy women was finishing a *zambra* dance, the guitar picking up her provocative movements with a syncopated beat, the music more Moorish than classically Spanish. Guests were calling out verbal encouragements of *"Anda, anda . . . qué mujer más guapa . . . baila, baila, reina de mi vida."* Suddenly from the crowd came the low wailing of a singer, and this incited the dancer to a frenzy of swirls before beginning to strut, her hands over her head and her face lifted to the ceiling. The applause was endless, and Ellen hesitated in taking Amparo up to the guitarist until the room had quieted.

"Amparo, I didn't realize that you were supposed to dance here today."

"Well, I haven't mentioned it because . . . I

hoped . . . I hoped that my father would change his mind."

"If you really don't want to dance, Amparo, I could go up and speak to your father." She arched her neck to see if she could catch sight of Eric, who had momentarily disappeared. "Or, I could have Dr. Bradshaw speak to him."

"No, Ellen. I must dance. My mother used to perform a solo at every festival—before she went away. I have been dancing for her, you see. My father said it is my duty."

The guitarist motioned to them to approach the platform area. Ellen walked along with Amparo, thinking how she could save the child from a chore that seemed to be distasteful to her. She looked frantically through the crowd to try and catch a glimpse of Eric, but he was still nowhere in sight. Then she saw Joaquin standing quietly at the opposite end of the tent to the stage. He was looking down at the ground, his hands clasped behind his back, seemingly serious in thought. She couldn't attract his attention through the crowds of people and there would be no time to walk over to him as she and Amparo were now nearing the platform.

"Don't worry, señorita, I'm not too upset about performing," the child said as she placed her hand on Ellen's arm for reassurance.

"Amparo, if you really don't want to . . ."

"No . . . I'm ready, señorita," she answered as she climbed onto the stage.

As Amparo took her position in the center of the platform, the guitar began strumming the

Sevillana, a light and fluttery piece of music, which was usually performed, as Ellen remembered, by two couples. Now Amparo was beginning to execute the woman's role as a solo, waving her arms gracefully and then bending and dipping in swooping movements.

Madama was beaming in haughty pleasure as the child continued the dance of the region. As Ellen turned to look in Joaquin's direction, she saw that although the young landowner was watching his daughter dance, the expression on his face was angry, almost explosive. Looking back at the child, she knew that Amparo was certainly doing the dance justice so Joaquin could not be angry over his daughter's lack of agility. She looked back at him again just in time to see him turn abruptly away from the stage and stalk out of the tent.

The child's talent merited all of the applause, and as Amparo left the stage, Ellen reached for her hand and pulled her toward her to extend what she felt was a much-deserved embrace.

"Amparo, I had no idea that you were such a good dancer," she said.

"Oh . . ." Amparo was breathless, "I have been dancing for a very long time. Mostly I enjoy dancing for my friends. I . . . never did feel comfortable dancing for so many people."

"It didn't appear that you were disturbed about anything, Amparo."

"Señorita?"

"Yes, Amparo?"

"I don't think that my father liked my dance very much."

"Why do you say such a thing, Amparo? You should have seen how proud your grandmother looked while you danced."

"But, Señorita, I'm not speaking about my grandmother. When I first walked onto the stage, I thought that I saw him standing at the back of the tent. And then after I danced awhile, I saw that he was gone."

"Nonsense, Amparo. Your father was there during all of your performance. He merely moved from the spot where you first saw him," she lied. "I must admit that he did dash out of the tent as soon as your dance was over. Amparo, you are old enough to realize that this festival is one of the grandest events in the region and a lot of planning must go into it."

"Yes, I realize that," answered the child, showing a sense of seriousness beyond her years.

"Well now, your father had to dash away to tend to something. But he enjoyed your dancing very much. I was watching the expression on his face as you danced."

"He did? You were?" The child jumped up and down with happiness and ended her glee by again tossing herself into Ellen's arms. She held the child very tightly, silently asking someone, anyone, everyone, to forgive her for lying to keep the child unaware of Joaquin Pedregal's resentment toward her. But how could Amparo fail to notice Joaquin's coolness and disinterest in her? It had become so obvious to herself in the short time that she was a guest at the villa, and yet Amparo had probably endured the situation for a few years.

Ellen caught sight of Madama approaching them, and she purposefully held Amparo in the embrace while the woman strutted over to them.

"Yes, my dear grandchild, you certainly deserve Miss Ross's pleasure over your dance," said the woman.

"It was . . . I enjoyed doing it, Grandmother."

"Of course you did, my dear," the woman cooed. "We have our obligations, child. We are Pedregals, and we must never back away from our responsibility to our name."

"No, Grandmother."

"Miss Ross, why are you craning your neck so? Who are you seeking?"

"Oh, I'm sorry, Madama. I was . . . you haven't seen Eric Bradshaw anywhere, have you?"

"No, indeed I have not," she answered. "Now if you would just stop doing that, I have something to discuss with you. Amparo, child, go about and play. Miss Ross, if we could just step outside of this noisy tent, I think we could hear each other better, or . . . should I say . . . understand each other," said the woman as she produced a wide grin, a rare sight to Ellen since her arrival.

The air outside of the tent was cool and crisp, and the sky had already taken on the dimness of early evening. Ellen felt invigorated and suddenly very happy. Eric, where are you, she wanted to cry out. Of course I'll marry you and live the rest of my days with you—and love you. Eric, where are you?

"Miss Ross," Madama's affected voice broke through her thoughts and quickly brought her down to the present. "Come, let us walk over toward the garden . . . where we could talk privately."

Neither of them spoke to each other as they strolled, although Madama did stop briefly once or twice to bid farewell to departing guests. Ellen was wary of what Madama had in mind to discuss. She was prepared for anything. The day had come and gone oddly, she mused. She had never expected Joaquin to participate in the *corrida*. Eric was correct in saying to her that she had been spending too much time in the library and seeking hidden passages and doting over the lovely tower retreat of Lucinda Pedregal. And when she did see Joaquin in action, she was surprised but pleased at his agility and knowledge of the bulls. Then came Eric's proposal—yes, he had meant what he said. He was not teasing her. He did want her to marry him. And if only she could find him, she would tell him yes, yes, yes, she would be his wife.

She wanted all of this to be over, to leave the Pedregal estate with Eric, and to continue her own life. She would never forget the villa. After all, it was the place where she met Eric. Yet she was weary of the complications surrounding the Pedregal family. She was sorry for Amparo, very sorry for the child—although Amparo had her whole life ahead of her and could still find happiness. Perhaps she was sorrier for Madama and most of all for Joaquin who had allowed an empty sense of priorities to rule their lives.

"I think we can talk here, Miss Ross," the woman said.

They had stopped in the garden by the rose trellises. She was happy that they hadn't stopped near the jasmine bushes. She had always connected the jasmine petals and their aroma with happiness.

"Yes, Madama," was all she answered.

"Miss Ross. I find that you are quite fond of Amparo. Is that not true?"

"Of course I am, Madama. She's a bright little girl with a good head on her shoulders. She's also very sweet and loving," no thanks to you, she wanted to add.

"Do you realize what this estate means to the child—or shall I say—*will* mean to her when she is grown?"

"I . . . don't understand," she murmured. What was this woman getting at? she asked herself.

"Amparo's mother is dead. This you know. I . . . am on in my years. And Joaquin . . . well, she will only have Joaquin in a short while. As an only child, she needs the security of this estate for her future. Do you understand what I am saying, Miss Ross?"

"I understand what you're saying, but I don't know how all this applies to me," she answered.

"Miss Ross, tomorrow evening we are holding a small dinner party and dance at the villa for our closest friends. It would be an appropriate time for Joaquin to make the announcement of the authenticity of the Perez paintings and the transfer of them to Don Antonio. Now, wouldn't that be grand, Miss Ross?"

"Grand, Madama?"

"You have not come up with any of the documents, have you?"

"No . . ."

"Well, no matter. When my husband passed on, some papers of his were never found. These documents are not necessary. Surely you can see that the paintings are Perez originals. You know, Miss Ross, their sale to Don Antonio will mean a lot to this estate, and in turn to Amparo—and also to you."

"I don't follow you, Madama."

"Of course we are planning to compensate you well for all the extra work you've done in searching our shelves for the documents. All of this was not in your regular line of duty, and I am aware of that."

"But I agreed to do it when I took the assignment."

"Nonsense, child. Just think. If you authorize the authenticity of the Perez paintings without further delay or testing, you will be securing Amparo's future and, most important, your own. Think about it, Miss Ross," she said snidely as she walked away from the girl.

Ellen stood where she was and followed Madama's departure with her eyes. The woman was afraid of having her test the artwork. She had taken her aside to bribe her, depending upon her feelings for the child, to help persuade her to give a positive result to the authentication of the paintings.

Ellen sighed deeply as she made her own way toward the villa. It had surely been an odd day, she thought, and after this latest with Madama, she felt sure that nothing more could possibly happen before day's end.

CHAPTER 13

The white flamenco outfit was strewn over the chaise, and as Ellen fastened the tie on her robe, she made her way over to the opened window that faced the gardens and the rolling fields behind the house. The moon was a bright crystal ball that lit the grounds as if it were early dusk. The terrain was a deep, velvet green groomed and fussed over, and the land, most of it Pedregal owned, ran for acres around the villa. The silver branches of the olive trees glittered in the moonlight, and the intermittent squares of red, plowed dirt and grass shone like nature's patchwork quilt over the earth.

She wondered then why Madama could not be content with all that she had—the beautiful villa, the gardens, the ranch, and the land—without asking for more. Half of the woman's jewels placed on the seller's block would bring in ample funds to keep the family going for years into the future. The other half of Madama's jewels, after her demise, would give Amparo financial security on into her marriage.

But Madama wanted more, so urgently that she was willing to bribe Ellen to authenticate the Perez paintings without even testing them. She wondered then if the search for the documents—an endeavor that always seemed quite unnecessary to her—was just a front to precipitate a delay in looking at the paintings themselves. Joaquin had told her not to touch the artwork until she really had to. First she must look for the documents, he had said. That is the way he wanted it handled. And in the meantime—he also bribed her, offering her love and happiness. His false attempt at romancing her was indeed obvious, she mused. In fact, she thought, he wasn't even interested enough in the game to carry it forth for very long. He had always been cordial enough to her, though his attempts at pursuing her more personally were quick, without depth, and easily distracted. It was very obvious why both he and Madama had commissioned someone out of their realm of acquaintances and far from their area of residence to study the artwork. They were relying on bribery from the outset. Why, then, were they so sure that the paintings were not authentic? And if they did assume that they were copies, how could they pawn these off on poor Don Antonio? The ranch owner was anxious to acquire these as a gift for his daughter, but she doubted that he would accept anything but authentic work. And yet would he really know if he were given copies of the great Cordobés painter? Excellent copies would fall so close that only the trained eye could detect the truth, and most of the time testing had to be performed to make an honest appraisal.

Ellen sighed as she leaned farther out on her window ledge. She loved the feeling of the crisp Andalusian air on her face. The festival area to the left now looked like a deserted carnival village with only the ghostly echoes of laughter resounding in the wind that rustled through the trees. A few guests had lingered on into the early evening, but finally even they—exhausted from the dancing and celebrating—had deserted the tents, leaving only the gypsy singers to continue their wailing, as if holding a private festival of their own. Now everyone was gone, and the gaiety that had resounded through the grounds that day, was put to rest—probably as circumstances went at the villa—until another year came to pass.

It was festival's end, a time that should have provided final answers to many of the situations at the villa. Yet everything was still disjointed.

Eric had vanished, nowhere to be found since late afternoon. Joaquin was angry and disturbed and even more resentful of Amparo than Ellen had ever seen him. Madama had added more intrigue to the day by telling her that she expected Joaquin to announce the authenticity of the Perez paintings and their transfer to Don Antonio the following evening at the small dinner party and dance to be held at the villa. And she herself further complicating the picture had not announced her findings to anyone at the house. Someone knew that she had been tugging at the painting on the landing that night when she was struck on the head. From afar it could have been observed that she was straightening the painting on its wall hanging. Yet no one would strike her for merely balancing a crookedly hung painting. They had to surmise that she was trying to gain access to the beautiful tower retreat of Lucinda Pedregal. She assumed that her final visit to the tower suite to test the Vargas painting was left undetected. With the knowledge that she had gained there and the actual testing of the Perez paintings, she had a wealth of information that she was keeping to herself. She was uneasy about harboring this information and not sharing it with anyone—especially Eric. Yet she had vibes that she could not explain that told her to wait. Basically she wanted the Pedregals to resolve the situation without placing herself as catalyst in determining the future of the family.

Her reflections were interrupted suddenly as her eye caught movement in the garden below. At first she couldn't determine who it was, and then the figure walked past the rose trellises and jasmine bushes to stand and look out across the fields that she had previously been viewing. It was Eric Bradshaw.

No time was wasted before she was out on the landing and making her way down the staircase, across the patio, and through the door that gave access to the garden. Her happiness over seeing him could not be contained, and she called out his name even before she reached him. As he turned abruptly toward her, she did not have to continue her steps to see the expression of anger on his face.

She stopped completely then, and called, "Eric . . . what . . . where . . . I've been searching for you all day."

"Have you?" he answered as he looked directly at her.

She continued walking toward him now. "Did you leave the festival completely?"

"I . . . didn't feel very much like celebrating the afternoon away," he answered.

She was disturbed even more as his expression of anger changed to one of disappointment.

"Amparo . . . danced very well. She was a little shaky about going on, but she was soon swept into the swing of things. Her performance was excellent," she said, trying to soften his mood.

"I'm happy about that. Madama was pleased, I imagine?"

"Yes, she was. And Joaquin . . . well, Joaquin disappeared after a while, and I never saw him again either."

There was silence as they stood and peered at each other.

"Eric?" She could not bear his mood any longer. "What did happen to you this afternoon? I was beginning to get frantic."

He didn't answer her at first, and then, "I . . . was looking for secret passages," he said coolly.

"I don't understand."

"Oh, I think you do. I was looking for the same secret passage that you evidently found a while ago. The one that you decided not to tell me about."

"Now it's you who doesn't understand," she said.

"Oh, I think I do now. At first I couldn't quite

comprehend what you were doing at the far end of the landing late at night when you were struck. And when you commented that you were looking for a hidden passage, I thought you were ribbing me. Then it suddenly came to me."

"Eric, please."

"No, let me continue. The document that I was searching for had to be kept in a place other than the library. In the time that I've stayed here, I've searched every nook and cranny in every part of the house that is visible. Oh, yes, I even entered Joaquin's bedroom when he was away and searched through his papers like a thief—that's how important all this is to me."

"And you found nothing?"

"Of course I found nothing," he snapped. "Then it suddenly all came together. Many of these old houses have closed-off nooks and passages that were used a few hundred years ago for odd and sundry purposes. The idea came to me during the festival as I looked up at the tall silo. There had to be some other place that I hadn't searched and it had to be the top of the tower. Also, the access to it had to be on the landing where you were struck."

"Listen, Eric, I didn't even look for your document in there. I had no time."

"Let me finish. When I reached the landing this afternoon after taking leave of you, I realized there could be only one access to the tower from that spot, and the large painting was the key. I merely moved it and found the stairway."

"And you found the document?" she asked. "Eric, I didn't even look for . . ."

"No, there was no document. But I did see the painting of the bouquet of flowers. I imagine you already studied it. What is it, a late Gauguin?" he said snidely.

"No, it's not, but it is quite valuable. Eric, all that is not important to me now. It's you that . . ."

"Well, it is important to me. I ask you again, Ellen. Have you ever trusted anyone in your life? Would you ever trust me? I imagine you've already tested the Perez paintings?"

"Yes, I have. Eric, do you realize that the information I have been withholding—and I've only had all the answers for twenty-four hours, not longer—can change the future of the Pedregal family. I've hesitated in divulging everything with the hope that Joaquin . . ."

"With hope that Joaquin will see the light and confess everything? Don't be naive, Ellen. And—I imagine that they offered you something as well."

"Well, as a matter of fact, Madama did . . ."

"I thought so," he interrupted. "Ellen, how could you?"

"Now it's you who mistrusts me, Eric. I was going to divulge everything tonight."

"And . . . I haven't heard anything to the effect that you've made any announcements on the situation."

"Well, I haven't. You had disappeared, and Joaquin couldn't be found."

"So, taking the easy road, you continue to withhold the information?"

"Eric, be understanding of what I had in mind."

"I don't know what you had in mind. And, Ellen, at this point I don't really care," he snapped as he brushed past her and walked toward the roadway that led to his chalet.

The walk back to the villa seemed endless. Her head throbbed as a result of all that had occurred. She remembered faintly that it was she who commented not more than a few hours before that nothing more could take place that day.

She had walked through the patio and as she began to climb the tall staircase, she felt the tears stinging against her cheeks.

"Jim Bradley," she said aloud but softly, "why did you send me here? I won't allow you to do this to me again. I just won't."

Her ascent of the staircase was slow and labored, and at every step she pulled herself up with a firm grip on the banister.

Why didn't he understand? she asked herself. Why couldn't he see that she wanted to give Joaquin a chance and the family an opportunity to come together. He had called her naive. Perhaps she was. Ultimately she would have announced her findings. She had planned to announce them after the festival if Joaquin hadn't come around before then. Of course he didn't come forth on his own. Things were worse instead of better between Joaquin and Amparo. Madama had further discouraged her by bribing her to give affirmative authentication of the artwork. Yes, she was naive, she agreed.

As she neared the top of the staircase, she could hear heated conversation emanating from Madama's quarters. The female voice was that of the older woman, of that she was sure. The other voice was that of a gentleman. Was it Eric Bradshaw? But she saw him walking toward the road. It couldn't be the doctor. Had he retraced his steps to confront Madama with the situation?

She made her way quietly over to the doorway of Madama's suite and placed her ear against the door jamb. She had never done anything like that before in her life. But she had to know.

"It's useless; we should forget all of this, Mother," the man's voice said.

"How can we, Joaquin? Just think, my son, of what we will be giving up. We are on the brink of solidifying our assets for the future. Think of Amparo, think of yourself."

"I am thinking of Amparo. But you're not, are you, Mother?"

"What do you mean by that statement?" The haughtiness of her tone reached Ellen without mistake.

"You're thinking of yourself, as you always have. The duenna of the Pedregal estate. That was always the most important thing to you, even when my father was alive."

"How could you say that to me?"

"Because it's true. Let's have no dishonesty between the two of us. We know each other too well."

"And you? Have you not gloried in the Pedregal name?" her voice lashed.

"Oh, I've had a good life. Materially I have lacked nothing."

"And what do you imply by that?" was her comeback.

"I enjoyed the ranch, Mother. I loved the bulls, even as a child. If only I could have remained a matador. I had the finesse with them. You saw me this afternoon, did you not?"

"Yes, I saw you triumph, and then, as always, instead of enjoying the glory, no one could find you. Joaquin, my son, you never really enjoyed the honor of being a Pedregal as much as you could have. Right now you are hesitating over the development and expansion of the land. You are going to let this fall through your fingers."

"I cannot do anything dishonestly."

"Nonsense! You had that girl in the palm of your hand when she first arrived here. And then you let it drop, cold."

"She is a lovely girl . . . I just couldn't . . ."

"You couldn't because your mind is still on that woman."

"That woman, as you call her, was my wife, Mother."

"She was a nobody. She brought you nothing. She was from mediocre stock."

"And yet it's with her land that you want to make us the greatest family in all the region."

"We are the greatest family," Ellen heard the woman snap. "The land is important to secure your future and Amparo's. But it will make us nothing more than we are already. The Pedregals have always been on top. You are not even thinking of your own daughter. You must go through with this."

"I suppose you are right, after all," he sighed.

"I have already spoken to that girl—that Ellen. Do you realize that her family sold their estate, and when they did own an estate, they had no servants? Only a gardener came once a week, Miss Ross said. When I heard that, I knew I could . . . shall we say, interest her in being repaid for extra work done in looking for the document."

"Mother, you didn't."

"Hush now. Looking for the documents was beyond her realm of duty. She should be recompensed."

Ellen heard Jóaquin's laughter. "Wouldn't it be amusing, Mother, if the Perez paintings were real after all?"

"Nonsense. If your father purchased authentic Enrique Perez artwork, he would have hung them immediately. Instead we found them below in his workshop buried under a lot of other debris."

"Perhaps he was hiding them, Mother," was Joaquin's retort.

"Hiding them? From whom?"

"Could it be that he was hiding them from you? Perhaps he knew that you would soon sell them in exchange for . . . jewels, land, a summer chalet at the newest resort? No, that last you would never do. You would never leave this estate. You love it too much."

"And you should love it too, Joaquin. Don't

throw this opportunity away. Talk to that Miss Ross tomorrow. Do anything you have to. She must authenticate the artwork."

"Mother, it will be as you wish. It has always been as you wished. I'm tired now. I'm going to bed."

"Come, kiss me good night, Joaquin," said his mother.

Ellen lost no time in leaving her position at Madama's apartment door. Instead of continuing on the landing to her own room, however, with quick but light movements, she made her way down the staircase and turned in the direction of the side door. She turned behind the stairwell just as she heard Joaquin leaving his mother's apartment. She waited until she heard the door of his own room open and close. Then she was out the side door and running through the garden and toward the roadway that led to Eric Bradshaw's chalet. Eric was right, she said to herself. How could she have been so naive. She had wanted Joaquin to make amends for all of his plotting and Madama's scheming. She had wanted him to unravel things—to put everything right on his own. In this way, the family could go on and live without embarrassment—which is what would happen if she confronted them and exposed the ruse. Now, after hearing the conversation between mother and son, she knew that nothing could be done for either Madama or Joaquin. She should not have been so naive in the beginning. She should have confided in Eric Bradshaw. After all, it was he whom she loved.

She turned off the road now and decided to take a shortcut through the grounds of the chalet. It would be faster, and she was anxious to speak to the doctor.

Just as she was about to leave the densest part of the garden, she saw someone come out from the front side of the chalet. She craned her neck to try to distinguish who the person was. The light shining through the living room windows now illuminated the figure and she stepped back in quiet amazement as she realized that the figure leaving Eric Bradshaw's chalet was Louisa, the Pedregals' housekeeper.

She watched the girl walk down the center path of the chalet and out onto the main roadway.

Ellen crept deeper into the hedges so that her presence would not be detected. Then, only as the housekeeper entered the servants' entrance of the main house, did Ellen relax enough to step onto the lawn of the blue stucco house.

She hesitated only for a few minutes, and then turned abruptly and made her way back to the villa.

As she entered her own room, she remembered again her thoughts of early evening when she felt that nothing more intriguing could possibly happen before day's end.

CHAPTER 14

There were many things to accomplish that day. First she would find Joaquin and make a clean declaration of all that she knew from the testing of the Perez paintings. She would also admit to Joaquin that she had stumbled upon his wife's tower suite and ask him if he were aware of the fact that the suite housed a very valuable work of Guintanilla Vargas. Then she would ask Felix to ready the carriage to take her to town so that she could make arrangements with the airline office for transportation out of Spain. She wouldn't take the train north to Madrid this time. That would take too long. The train would give her too many hours to think, to remember, to regret. The plane would lift its wheels off the ground at the Seville airport and not touch down until Lisbon. At least it wouldn't be Spain, where the earth was red like a new copper penny and the foliage was lush and sweet smelling and intoxicating. Yes, she was becoming sentimental already—all the more reason to get away as soon as possible. Perhaps she should leave that afternoon. What reason would she have to wait there another night? Surely attending the gala would not be reason enough. Her work was done, her responsibilities over. There was no need to stay any longer.

She had been lolling in bed, looking up at the

ornately carved ceiling. The room they had assigned her had been pleasant. In thinking further, if she had arrived at the villa and kept to her own business, she could have come away feeling that she had enjoyed her assignment. Her accommodations had been pleasant, and Seville was a lovely city steeped in history and quite charming. The Pedregal festival had been exciting. She had never seen a bullfight before, and Joaquin had performed very well. The festivities of gypsy singing and dancing had intrigued her. She had even dressed for the occasion by donning a white flamenco dress and lace mantilla. Yes, everything would have turned out quite well, except that she had fallen very deeply in love. It had been the last thing she had in mind when she left the States. She had begged Jim Bradley to send her on this assignment so that she could rest her mind over the torment she had felt at her break with Sandy. She had wanted distraction and new surroundings. It would all have been perfect if she hadn't fallen in love with Eric Bradshaw. And she would not have felt so deeply for Eric if she had not become involved with the family situation there.

Yet they had all pushed her into involvement. They had brought her to the threshold of all the intrigue and complications. And once immersed in all this, she had come to know the people there, and then she had slowly but steadily become involved with them. She felt compassion toward Amparo, pity for Madama and Joaquin, and love for Eric. And the problems of these people had weighed heavily on her shoulders as she tried to sort them all out and amend them.

She began to dress then, her movements slow and labored. In all of her compassion for these people, she thought, the one she had shown least understanding for was the doctor. And actually his cause had been the most honest and altruistic of them all. Although she had not seen the document or the letter written by Lucinda, she knew how dedicated the doctor was in trying to establish a clinic in the area for the children. Ultimately that was the important factor to consider. Yet she had wanted the Pedregal family to benevolently offer the land toward this goal. Yes, she was naive. She wanted everything to turn out well in the end. But, life is not like that, and she had been foolish in thinking that it was. There was nothing else left for her to do but leave.

She made her way down the stairway and walked over to the *antesala* for breakfast. The house seemed quiet, and the trickle of water spouting from the fountains seemed to echo through the patio and breakfast room. The family members were probably sleeping late after the previous day of exhausting festivities. Yet it was on into the morning, and surely Felix or Louisa should be about.

As if summoned by a mental beckoning the housekeeper appeared at the doorway just then. Her presence had no apparent motive other than to stare at the girl who was seated at the dining table. Having become used to her gaping, Ellen took advantage of the situation by asking her the few things she had to know.

"Louisa, good morning."

"Señorita," the other girl nodded.

"I must see Joaquin at once. Could you tell me where he could be found?"

"I'm sorry, Miss Ross," she said more coolly than usual. "Señor Joaquin has gone for the day. He has taken Amparo and said that he would return late this afternoon."

"He's taken Amparo?" Ellen stammered.

"What is so odd about that, señorita? He is her father," she snapped.

"Yes, well . . . it's just that . . . I wanted to speak to him this morning." She didn't know why, but she felt uneasy about Amparo being with Joaquin for so long a time away from the villa. From the lack of attention he had given the child all the while Ellen had stayed there, it seemed odd that he should take her on an excursion now. "No matter," she continued, "I'll speak to him when he returns. Instead, would you ask Felix to prepare the carriage. I would like to go to town. If he's busy, tell him, if you would, that I could drive it myself."

"As you wish, señorita," the other girl said as she walked out of sight.

Ellen felt almost like shivering from the coolness that had emanated from the housekeeper. She wouldn't dote on it, however. The girl never liked her from the first moment that she arrived at the house.

She tarried a little longer over her coffee to give

Felix a chance to prepare the carriage. In a way she hoped she would be taking the rig by herself. She thought a lot of Felix, but in her present mood she would prefer to be alone on the trip to town.

She reflected again over Louisa. She had tried not to let her mind jump to the scene in Eric's garden the night before. Yet she could not lie to herself. She had seen Louisa coming from the front door of the doctor's chalet. She clenched her fists tightly as she felt the hurt that all this had brought to her. Was he so fickle that just a few hours after their argument he was able to forget her completely and invite Louisa to his chalet? Or perhaps it wasn't fickleness but anger or disillusionment over the fact that she had not trusted him enough to level with him concerning her findings in the tower. She had not imagined Louisa walking from Eric's chalet. She blinked very hard to keep the tears away. Louisa had been with Eric the previous night, there was no way to get around it. But she wouldn't judge him now, or place the blame on herself for driving him to it. The situation had become too complicated, and she had no extra energy to put the pieces back together again.

She rose from the table and started walking through the patio toward the front of the house. Felix had had ample time to prepare the rig. She tarried a few minutes as she came to the center of the garden. The tarpaulin had already been unraveled across the top of the patio to keep the warmest rays of sun away from the sitting area. In summer the tarpaulin would stay this way for most of the daylight hours. On a day like this one Felix would roll it back after lunchtime. Now the days began with a cool crispness, and ended the same. But the midday sun still had some strength to it as if summer were reluctant to make its final exit.

The carriage was waiting for her in front of the house. Felix held the reins for her as she settled herself in the rig. The old man was full of apologies that he could not drive her himself and tried to persuade her to wait until afternoon. She decided not to mention to him that she was headed for the airline offices. She would have to ask for reservations that morning if she planned to leave by nightfall. She would need the afternoon to pack and speak to Joaquin.

She started off slowly down the main roadway using all of her willpower not to look in the direction of Eric's chalet as she passed. She kept a steady pace all the way to town, thanking her younger summers spent on a country farm for enabling her to manage the rig.

The airline offices were part of the shopping area attached to the Cristina Hotel. There was always adequate space provided at the side of the hotel for carriages to be left, as many of the families who lived on the outskirts of Seville or in the San Juan de Aznalfarache district preferred to use these in place of automobiles when traveling to town.

Ellen secured her reins on the post provided for this and was turning the corner in front of the hotel when she heard her name being called. Turning, she was surprised to see Don Antonio approaching her.

"Miss Ross, what a pleasant surprise. Is Joaquin with you?"

"Good morning, Don Antonio. This certainly is a surprise. No, Joaquin . . . was away from the estate when I left. I . . . I'm here to do some shopping."

"Ah, yes. These stores are quite elegant here." There was silence for a few moments, and Ellen noticed that Don Antonio was preoccupied in thought. Then, "Miss Ross, will you stop with me a few moments. There's an outdoor café just around this corner, almost adjacent to the shops. Just a few minutes, Miss Ross. I know you're anxious to pursue your shopping. We'll just stop for a cup of coffee."

"Yes, well, if you wish, Don Antonio."

He took her arm and led her in silence to the other side of the hotel. There, as he predicted, was the small outdoor café, and adjacent to that a series of six stores—one of them housing the airline office.

They sat at a small table near the edge of the hotel, which was shaded by a few palm trees. The front grounds of the hotel were filled with an abundant number of these trees, and Ellen found the surroundings very pleasing. A quick thought came to mind that she should have booked a room at the Cristina Hotel and commuted to the villa each day to do her work. Everything might have been different if she had, she mused.

Don Antonio had clapped his hands to summon the waiter and after asking for two orders of *café con leche* and two *tapas* of *ensalada*, the older man folded his hands on the table in front of him and looked directly into the girl's eyes.

"Miss Ross, I will not waste your time but get right to the point."

Ellen froze a little as she wondered if the man was about to ask her information that she could only reveal to Joaquin Pedregal.

"Go on, Don Antonio."

"Miss Ross, Don Pedregal, Joaquin's father, was my closest friend. Yet although we were close, we respected each other's privacy. Therefore in one way I feel that if Don Pedregal had acquired two Perez paintings before he died, he would have told me. In another way there are many treasures, I may call them that, which he owned and which I own that we never discussed. Therefore it is also not odd that I never saw the paintings until they hung in the villa after his death."

"Don Antonio, what you are trying to say," Ellen asked quietly, "is that you doubt the authenticity of the artwork?"

"No, Miss Ross. It's going to be a shock to you, but what I'm trying to say is that I don't care about the authenticity of the paintings."

"I don't understand."

"It's really all very simple. Don Pedregal's estate and mine were both very much the same in land and cattle. I do have a few acres more of land and a few extra head of cattle than he had. The great difference in our holdings, Miss Ross, is

that I've always had more ready capital on hand
than Don Pedregal. Doña Elena, my wife . . . well
. . . her wants were always . . . simple, let us say."

"And Madama's more extravagant, Don Antonio?"

"Well. . . ." The man blushed as a gentleman would have at that moment.

"What I'm trying to say, Miss Ross, is that I
have been trying to help the Pedregals since
Joaquin's father's death. But they are a proud
family. I know the development of the adjacent
land means so much to them. Poor Joaquin has
had his troubles. And Madama . . . this woman
came from humble beginnings in Granada. But,
even so, she has done a good job as duenna of the
Pedregal estate. I know that the land development
would make her feel . . . good also."

"What is it that you are asking, Don Antonio?"
Ellen asked.

"Don Pedregal helped me one day many years
ago. I would like to do his family a good turn
now. I would love to own two authentic Perez
paintings to give to my daughter. Yet . . . if they
were not authentic Perez paintings . . . I would
not mind purchasing them anyway under the pre-
tense that they were authentic."

Ellen was aghast. Don Antonio did not mind
being defrauded.

"I know . . . you think I am mad. But, don't
you see, that is the only way I would be able to
give the Pedregals some ready cash, being that
they are so proud," he sighed.

"But . . . Madama," she stammered. No, she would not tell him. She could not.

"Oh, yes. You think Madama is not worth all of this. Miss Ross, Madama was always a good woman. A little too false on the haughtiness . . . but she was always a good woman. She became desperate after Don Pedregal's death. She tried to hold on to her position, trying very hard not to return to the poverty she knew as a child. You must understand these things."

"But her jewels?"

"Let the woman have her jewels, Miss Ross. She lost so much when Don Pedregal died."

"Don Antonio, I . . . must leave you now. I understand what you are saying. Joaquin will be speaking to you tonight at the gala. I assume you will be there?"

"Oh, yes. Yes, I will be present." He looked at her hesitantly.

"I must say, Don Antonio, that you are a very fine man. I do hope the Pedregals appreciate you."

He smiled at her, seemingly content that he did not offend her by his request. She knew that he was watching her as she made her way over to the airline office.

She fastened the belt of the deep-aqua-print silk and looked at herself one more time in the mirror behind her dresser. Then she decided that she had a few things to say to the image in the mirror.

"Ellen Ross, you are a very shallow person," she

said aloud. "Here you have been despising Madama Pedregal the entire time you've been here, not even stopping to think that the poor woman might have had her own troubles at one time. And," she continued, "Don Antonio, the insignificant, but wealthy landowner who you thought was just anxious to get his hands on the Perez paintings has turned out to be a very altruistic gentleman. Perhaps Eric Bradshaw was right, Miss Ross," she continued addressing herself. "Perhaps you are a very mistrusting, skeptical person indeed."

Although she couldn't condone Madama's intent to defraud, she suddenly felt very sorry for all of them. Most of all she felt sorry for herself. Because there were no tickets available by air out of Seville for two days, she was forced to witness the gala that evening and the outcome of the situation at the villa. It almost turned out as she hoped—with everyone being content—but of course someone would go away disappointed. She feared very strongly that the disappointment would fall on Eric Bradshaw. That is the one main reason why she wanted to be far away from there that evening. She wouldn't worry about Don Antonio—he would be happy just to have an excuse to give the Pedregals some financial assistance. And Joaquin would have the Vargas painting and the other two works of art to do with what he liked. And since Joaquin would naturally sell all the paintings, Madama would have her land developed. Yes, it would be only Eric Bradshaw who would walk away disappointed. And she, Ellen

Ross, would walk away in another direction, saddened and heartbroken.

She could not mention Lucinda's document to Joaquin. She would mention the Vargas painting because she saw that and appraised it. Perhaps that would give Joaquin incentive to confess all. But she doubted that Joaquin would say anything that would not benefit himself and the estate. Unless . . . Eric Bradshaw could cause a scene, she thought. But he wouldn't.

She gave one final brushing to her hair, as if procrastinating the journey down to the patio and the gala. Her retribution for being such a mistrusting individual, she mused, was to attend the party. She wondered if Eric Bradshaw would be there.

CHAPTER 15

As she closed the door to her room and began descending the stairs, she gave a worried thought to Amparo and Joaquin. Madama and Louisa had been frantic just before they all went upstairs to dress late that afternoon. The young landowner and his daughter had not yet reappeared from their outing. Now as she arrived in the patio and as if reading Ellen's thoughts, Madama came sweeping up to her with an equally worried look on her face.

"Miss Ross, cocktails are being served in the *antesala*. You haven't . . . you haven't seen Amparo or Joaquin, may I ask?"

"No, Madama," she answered. "Where could they have gone?" she queried, her voice showing her nervousness.

"I don't know," the woman said, obviously bordering on panic.

"Madama, I want to ask you something," Ellen said, trying to control her voice.

"What is it, Miss Ross, I have no time now to . . ."

"Madama, could there be anything really wrong, I mean dangerously wrong with Joaquin keeping Amparo away this long?"

The old woman just stared at her for a few moments. Then, "Miss Ross, Joaquin loves that child.

Oh, I know it appears that he's cooled toward her recently, but that is only because the child reminds him so much of Lucinda. It tears his heart every time he looks at her to remember that Lucinda is gone. I am frantic that he is not here because he is disrupting my party. I knew this moment would come, this renewal of his show of love for her—a love that was always there. But why today? Do you realize that the guests are all here, Miss Ross?" She bristled and then turned in the direction of the *antesala*.

Holding back a chuckle to herself, Ellen called out, "Madama, is Eric Bradshaw here yet?"

"No, he isn't. He sent word by Milta that he would be delayed. He was also away today. Everyone has left me here with no consideration . . ."

Ellen could not hear the end of Madama's lamentations as the woman disappeared in the direction of the *antesala*.

She stood a moment alone in the patio thinking about what Madama had said. Again Ellen Ross had been mistrusting, she said to herself. What was she thinking that Joaquin was up to by not returning earlier with Amparo. The child had no bearing on the Vargas painting or the land. There would be no reason to harm her. "Ellen Ross, what have you turned into?" she asked aloud as she walked toward the *antesala*.

The room, though small, was filled with people. Ellen caught sight of Don Antonio in the opposite corner and nodded to him, although there were too many people between them to make conversational contact at that moment. Instead she walked over to the buffet which had been turned into a bar and helped herself to a cool drink. She noticed Louisa passing hors d'oeuvres from one guest to another. She knew no one else in the room.

In one instance she was relieved that Eric Bradshaw had not arrived. Yet in the same thought she did want to see him, fleetingly, before she left. This would be a good opportunity to catch a glimpse of him among all these people without having to engage in personal conversation. Perhaps she wouldn't see him at all. She doubted that she would stay for the dance after dinner. If he did not show by that time, they might not run into each other again before she left in two days. He was probably covering as much ground as possible throughout the south, soliciting funds for his clinic. Perhaps he would be able to acquire enough revenue to purchase land somewhere other than that adjacent to the estate. Of course it would take longer to solicit additional funds to purchase new land.

It was as she was reflecting on this that the sight appeared at the doorway—a shocking sight and yet one that was at the same time pleasing and natural.

Joaquin was dressed in the finest gray silk suit she had ever seen tailored. His shirt was a deep blue, and his tie was a small print of three deeper blues. On his arm he escorted the most beautifully groomed child she had ever seen. She was dressed in a very crisp blue voile with a very wide satin sash. Everyone in the room stopped their chatter as they could do nothing but stare at the magnificent sight the pair made in the doorway.

"Mother," Joaquin nodded at Madama. "And friends. You will forgive us." He looked down at Amparo, and they exchanged radiant smiles. "But now that we have interrupted you, we ask your indulgence for a few more moments as we have an announcement to make."

"Joaquin . . ." Madama stammered. "What are you up to?"

"Is Dr. Bradshaw here?" Joaquin asked, totally ignoring his mother.

"Dr. Bradshaw will be delayed," Louisa offered.

"Ah, too bad. Well, he will hear the good news when he arrives."

Ellen bit her lip. Could this be what she thought it was?

"Our very close friends are here tonight, Amparo, and it is fitting that we make this known at this time. We would like to tell all of you that on behalf of my beloved wife, Lucinda, and with wholehearted approval of my beautiful daughter and myself, the Pedregal family will donate the parcel of land at the far end of the estate to the medical profession for the purpose of building a clinic to help cure a particular children's blood disease. And," here he had to stop to make himself heard above the chatter that ensued from his announcement, "if you would allow me your attention a few more minutes. And the ground can be broken and building begun as a result of a contribution, which we shall put for sale, of a late painting by Guintanilla Vargas that belonged to my wife and that she requested be used for that purpose."

Ellen looked quickly over at Madama whose face had become ashen, but who was not uttering a word at that moment.

"Of course we will need additional funds, donations from everyone to help staff and equip the clinic. By the way, our own friend Dr. Eric Bradshaw will help direct all proceedings for the clinic."

Ellen took the opportunity to walk up to Joaquin at that moment and whisper in his ear.

"Well, the old scoundrel. My father was hiding those treasures of Perez paintings after all," he said quietly to Ellen. She smiled at him and stepped back so that he could continue speaking.

"My friends, I've just received additional good news. Miss Ross, the art appraiser who has been staying with us has just informed me that our two paintings of the Andalusian women are authentic originals of Enrique Perez. Don Antonio, I don't know if you are still interested . . ."

"Of course I am," Don Antonio called out. "I want those to give as a gift to my daughter. And, Joaquin, I'm also very interested in the Vargas painting. There is a certain little girl of about nine to whom I've always wanted to give a gift."

Joaquin looked down at Amparo and nodded, both of them beaming.

"I will tell you that all funds from the Vargas painting will go toward the clinic and the profits on one of the Perez paintings I will also donate to the clinic."

A cheer went up from the crowd of guests. Even Madama, looking at the enthusiasm of all her prominent friends, began to smile, and her face seemed to lose a little of its tenseness.

Suddenly Ellen felt someone tug at her arm, and looking up realized it was Louisa.

"This is all your doing, Miss Ross. But never you mind, I will put a stop to this," she said as she pushed Ellen aside and ran out of the room.

Without having to second-guess her, Ellen knew immediately what the girl was up to. However, in trying to regain her balance from the housekeeper's forceful push, she lost enough time to worry that she might be too late in preventing the disaster that was about to occur.

As soon as she regained her stance, she tore out of the room after the girl who was now at the top of the staircase and about to step onto the landing.

Ellen felt that she had never run so fast in all her life. Although Ellen scaled the steps two at a time, the housekeeper was enough ahead of her to foresee danger. Now as she moved the large painting at the end of the landing and walked through the opened panel, Ellen was just onto the landing at the top of the staircase. She's after the Vargas, she said to herself. She's going to damage Lucinda's painting.

The spiral stairs were awkward to climb under normal circumstances, but trying to scale them in large leaps was almost impossible. Yet she would not give up. Louisa must not damage Lucinda's painting. She would try with all her energy to stop the girl.

As she entered the beautiful tower suite, Ellen saw that Louisa was just raising her arms to take the Vargas bouquet from its hanging. There was no time to waste because the girl could just strike it over one of the posters of the bed, and it would be mutilated. There was no other way she said to herself, and without thinking further, she made one of the best tackles she had ever attempted. Now this was a sport that she hadn't gone near since she had her braces removed at the age of eleven. But before that time, and much to the dismay of her mother and sister, she always thought that her tackles were well timed and beautifully executed. If all that energy in practicing at that time was for no other moment than this one, it was well worth the jeers of her sister and the reprimand of her mother to be able to remember and execute the movement again at that time.

It was only after Louisa was on the carpeting, sputtering and complaining, that Ellen felt her ankle smart. She knew she had twisted it but could not dote any further on it. What the girl said next took her mind off it for a few minutes.

"I knew I should have found you the other night. The first blow to your head was not forceful enough. But I looked for you the other night and you were nowhere in the villa. I thought you were at Dr. Bradshaw's. I even peeked in the window of his living room, but you were nowhere in sight, and he was asleep on his divan."

"What . . . what are you saying?" Ellen gasped.

"I should have continued looking for you after that. I would have made short work of you. This is all your fault. I hated Lucinda. I hated his love for her," she spouted.

"Louisa. Do you mean that you were not in Eric Bradshaw's chalet the other night?"

"No. Evidently you were not there. Why should I have bothered him? I had no cause to disturb him."

"Ellen." Joaquin's voice interrupted the housekeeper, and as Ellen turned, she saw that Joaquin and Felix were leaning against the door frame of the room.

"We've heard everything. I couldn't imagine what was happening when Louisa pushed you and ran out and then you followed. Then Felix suggested what might be about to happen."

"Felix?" Ellen asked quietly.

"Yes, Ellen," Joaquin smiled. "You were not the only one waiting for a proper ending to all of this. Felix knew as much as you did. Since you surmised Louisa was coming here, I imagine you already discovered my wife's lovely hideaway suite?"

"Yes, I found it a while ago," she answered.

"And Eric. He was waiting for me to come to my senses?"

"Yes, I guess you can say that," she smiled.

"Felix and I will take Louisa downstairs and see that she is properly punished by the authorities for striking you. Are you coming?"

"I'll be down in a minute," she said, remembering her ankle and realizing that Louisa needed both Joaquin and Felix to contain her. Besides, she wanted a few moments to bid farewell to Lucinda Pedregal's beautiful room high above the clouds.

She made her way slowly down the spiral staircase, wishing with every few steps that she had allowed Joaquin and Felix to escort her down. Her ankle throbbed but it was not as unbearable as it was uncomfortable to balance herself on the narrow steps.

She was very happy for Joaquin that he was able to make the right decision about the land and the Vargas painting. She was also pleased that she was able to honestly authenticate the Perez paintings. Joaquin and Amparo looked so happy standing together as the announcement was made to the guests.

She had now reached the landing at the bottom of the spiral staircase. Before she rasied her hand to press the lever to open the panel—as someone had evidently forgotten that she was still in the tower and had closed it—she thought of the two days ahead of her and how long it would seem just waiting for the hour that her plane was to depart. She would rest in bed all the next day to cater to her ankle. Then perhaps in the evening she would pack in preparation for the next afternoon's flight.

Pleased at her projected schedule she raised her hand to push the lever. Nothing happened. She tried it again with similar results. Finally she panicked and beat the palm of her hand against the lever five or six times. There was silence.

She placed her forehead against the panel trying to decide whether to burst into tears or sink to the floor in utter exasperation.

"Someone, help, I'm locked in the passage," she yelled and she pounded her hand against the panel itself.

No one would hear her, she realized. The panel was too thick. She looked up along the height of the silo. She wouldn't perish from lack of oxygen, she guessed, as she could always toss her shoe against one of the tiny window slits to let more air penetrate the area. She wouldn't starve because eventually someone would remember where she was last seen and retrace their steps to the passage. But when? When would they come?

It was unfair, she thought. Unfair that her last hours at the villa should be spent in that predicament. Joaquin might even think she had gone to her room and he might not want to disturb her until the next day. She might not even be discovered until the following night.

It was when she felt the tears stinging against her face that she heard the lever of the panel click, and then as she looked further, the lever was beginning to move.

She exerted all of her remaining energy to pound forcefully against the panel. Placing her ear against the wood, she thought she heard a faint murmur of her name.

Suddenly the lever clicked again and the panel

opened leaving her face to face with a very serious-looking Eric Bradshaw.

"Eric! Eric, my foot, it's sprained. Oh, Eric, before I leaned too hard, I did nothing but lean. This time I was afraid to lean and trust at all. Neither was good, Eric. Joaquin made a full announcement of . . ."

She stopped, realizing the gush of disjointed information that was flowing out of her. They looked at each other, each studying the other for a few seconds.

"Did I say babbling, incoherent, and headstrong?" he said and then broke into one of the most attractive grins she had ever seen as he reached for her and brought her close into his arms. He kissed her tenderly, whispering his feelings to her while she clung to him urgently.

"Eric, where have you been? Did Joaquin tell you everything?" she finally said.

"Yes, he told me about the announcement. Actually, I spent the whole day at my chalet. I was going out of town, but then . . . well, to tell you the truth, I spent the day thinking how I could approach you to . . . well, I was wrong, Ellen. Joaquin had to be given the opportunity to get it all together on his own. I understand why you held off, Ellen. I was wrong in being hurt by what I thought was your lack of trust in me."

"But I'm not a trusting person . . . or I wasn't. I went from one extreme to the other. I need you, Eric. I need you to balance me. I need you to lean on—but not completely."

"Hush now," he said as he drew her to him

again. "I know you'll never lean on me completely, but I do want to take care of you somewhat. Would you let me do that, Ellen?" he asked her.

"Yes, Eric. But how much time we wasted."

"No, it was a learning process. We had to learn from ourselves where we were and how much we wanted. Ellen, I want you . . . very much. Do you think you will be able to last in Seville a few more years while I organize the clinic? We'll be married—oh, I'm sure the Pedregals will give us a blast of a party—and then we'll get our own apartment in Seville. Two years would do it. Would you agree to stay on here for two more years? You could get a leave from your museum."

"I would love to stay, Eric. I really haven't had too much time to relax and enjoy the surroundings without . . . without some trauma occurring."

"How is your foot? I'll bandage it when we get downstairs. Louisa was taken out of here for good. I'm surprised that her violence hadn't affected Amparo before this, but she usually kept away from the child, which was fortunate."

"But what about Madama? She was planning to defraud Don Antonio."

"Well, my own opinion is that Madama will be in her own private penance for the rest of her life. She will never see the estate expanded, although the profits of one Perez painting will be kept for family use, and with that the Pedregals will never want. No, she actually never committed fraud.

But you were the one that she bribed. Do you want to prefer charges?"

"No, I don't think so. There's malicious thought in all of us at times. I feel sorry for her, really."

"Well, I must say, she is making the best of it. She's down there now telling all of her guests the colors she plans to paint the clinic walls. And, oh yes, she says one room in the clinic must be a playroom filled to the brim with toys. I think Madama will survive."

"Joaquin and Amparo looked so grand in the doorway of the *antesala* as he made the announcement. Oh, Eric, I was so sorry you weren't there."

"He told me all about it when I came in. Poor chap had gone through such self-torment trying to make the right decision on what to do. He said he used to go up to the tower room at night and just reflect on his life with Lucinda and their love. He blames himself for being away a lot when she was ill. But he had to travel on family business once in a while. There was no one else but Joaquin to bear the burden."

"But where did he take Amparo today? They were gone so long."

"First he took her up to the tower room. He said that she remembered it from the times her mother took her there. Then he took her out into the country, and Felix secretly provided them with a picnic lunch so that they could stay as long as they liked. They needed time, Ellen, time to get reacquainted. Joaquin said that he told Amparo everything. He told her about her mother's will and about Madama's desires for the estate. They decided together what to do. Amparo even said that she would handle her grandmother if she protested too much. She said that her grandmother needed love and she would give it to her, and then she would feel better."

"Eric, I'm so pleased at how everything ended."

"It's not ended, Ellen. Everything is just beginning."

"Did I say contradictory?" She laughed as she tried to mimic him.

"Contradictory and in love," he said as he put his arm around her and began to lead her down the stairway.

From somewhere she thought she heard the music of a gypsy guitar. And as they reached the patio, the aroma of the jasmine flowers reached her—sweet and intoxicating like the evening that remained.